# RISING

WENDY SMITH

Edited by
LAUREN CLARKE

Cover Design by
BOOKISH GRAPHICS

BOOK TWO IN THE FALL AND RISE DUET

ISBN 13: 978-1-991303-34-9

**1**

———

COLE

My family.

They're like a magnet to me. Pulling me in even though I know I need to stay away and give Brooke space.

But I can't.

I sigh as I look up at Brooke's apartment. It's been six weeks since I helped her back to her apartment after her stint in hospital. Six weeks since she slammed the door in my face and on our relationship. I miss her and Kaia more than I can bear. Every day I feel myself drawn to this place, the memory of Brooke's warm body next to mine still fresh.

I want her.

I love her.

I need her.

Closing my eyes for a moment, I turn to walk away.

"Daddy."

I let out a loud breath and look back. Kaia runs straight at me, her arms open, and leaps as I kneel to receive her embrace.

"Hey, baby." I suck in a breath. She smells of strawberry shampoo. Her arms tighten around my neck.

"I miss you. Where have you been?"

I swallow hard. "I've been at my house."

"You don't sleep in Mommy's bed anymore?"

"Hi, Cole," Brooke says softly.

When I meet her gaze, I mourn that the love so recently in her eyes has gone. Her smile is small and strained. "Brooke."

Kaia cups my face and steers it back to her. "When are you coming to our place?"

I hate this. I'm about to break my little girl's heart. "I … I don't think I am. But you can come visit me sometime."

Her lower lip wobbles.

"Hey. If you ask Mommy nicely, maybe you can come and stay at my house for a night. We can do some decorating in your room."

Her head turns so fast, I'm amazed it doesn't fly off. "Can I, Mommy? You can sleep in Daddy's bed."

My heart's ripped from my chest at her words.

"I'll think about it." Brooke's tone's so cold, and I know it'll never happen. If I push, all that'll do is confirm her opinion of me.

*You can't take her from me.* Brooke's face, etched with panic, is still so fresh in my mind. Will she ever trust me again?

"Please, Mommy?"

"I said I'll think about it," she snaps, and I get a filthy look.

I press my lips to Kaia's cheek. "I have to get going. Be good for Mommy."

Kaia grabs my hand.

"Kaia, sweetheart." I force a smile. "I'll see you soon. I promise." Slowly, I pull my hand from hers and meet Brooke's cold gaze. "I just wanted to make sure you two were okay."

Brooke nods. "I appreciate it." She takes Kaia's hand. "Say goodbye to Cole."

"Goodbye, Daddy." Kaia hooks herself around Brooke's left leg. Her mouth is turned down into a pout.

With one last look, I turn away.

I hate this. I hate all of it.

I'm half the block away when I hear Kaia's voice.

"Daddy."

I keep walking. I can't stop. If I do, I risk losing both of them forever.

I'm shattered. I don't know if I can do this. I can't be what Kaia needs and not turn into the person Brooke fears.

When I reach the end of the street, I stop and catch my breath.

Whatever it takes, I'll win Brooke over again.

I have to.

For all our sakes.

**2**

---

BROOKE

Kaia cried for what felt like hours after we saw Cole.

She cried so hard, she was out like a light by the time I went to work.

Guilt wracks me when I have to leave her with Rosalyn. I have a heavy heart all the way to the bar.

There's more than enough money in my account for me to give up this job, and Cole is paying me child support every week, but it's the fear of the unknown that stops me from leaving. I'd love to have my evenings back with my little girl, but I'm scared of having the rug pulled out from under my feet.

Something happened between Cole and me. I don't know what it is, and it hurts that I can't remember. The agony on his face tells a story all of its own. But I can't bring myself to act on it.

I can't force myself to feel something for a man who walked away from me. Yet I'm keeping my family apart.

The night at work drags. My mind's on Kaia the whole time and how hard this is on her. I've always put her first, but maybe not this time. It's clear she loves Cole, and she knows him as her father. It's what leaves me in no doubt that I must have let him get close.

It's nearly midnight. I make myself a coffee to try and stay awake a little longer. While I'm feeling fine physically, it feels like there's a fog surrounding me.

There are no customers left, and I've got my things ready to go when it's time.

Craig tosses the dishtowel over his shoulder and puts the last glass back behind the bar. "Let me pack up, and I'll walk you home."

I'm not keen on walking by myself. Not after what happened. His suggestion fills me with a sense of relief.

The front door opens.

"Brooke."

I catch my breath. Damn Cole for looking so good. He's in a pair of dark jeans with a white button-up shirt. No tie. It feels familiar. "Cole? What are you doing here?"

"I wondered if you'd let me walk you home."

I flick a glance at Craig, and he shrugs. "Whatever you want."

Nodding, I pull on my jacket. I shouldn't. He left me when I needed him—he left both of us.

But something must have happened to make me let him in. For Kaia to let him in. And I owe it to her, if not to myself, to make sure she has a father.

"Okay. Let's go. See you tomorrow, Craig."

"See you tomorrow."

Cole holds the door while I walk out and onto the pavement.

"I wanted to say sorry about earlier. I hope Kaia was okay."

"She cried herself to sleep."

He sighs. "I just … well, I feel this need to check on you two. Things are so fucked up right now."

"I do appreciate it. We've all been through something. I just wish I could remember what."

"It's not your fault. What I want is to find the person who was chasing you and do the same to them. The thought of anyone hurting you …"

Why the hell does he tug at my heartstrings so much? Cole Masters hurt me more than anyone else has ever hurt me, but something made me give him another chance. "I didn't think you'd be outside today. I tried to pick a time when I knew Kaia wouldn't see me."

"We were late getting home."

"I hope you weren't late for work."

I shake my head. "It's fine. They're being really good since the accident."

"So they should be. They're lucky to still have you."

We walk together, but the distance between us is vast. Yet, having him by my side makes me feel safe.

I'm conflicted by the sorrow I feel when we reach my apartment.

"Thank you for walking me home." I give him a smile.

"Thank you for letting me. I wish …" He shakes his head. "Never mind. Have a good night."

"What is it?"

He shrugs. "I just wish things were back to the way they were before your accident. I miss you."

It hurts that I can't say the same.

"Good night, Brooke."

He leans over and pecks me on the cheek. Having him so close is surprisingly comforting, and for a moment, I don't want him to go.

"Get inside," he says.

I nod.

"I'll be there tomorrow night after your shift."

"Cole, you don't need—"

His dark eyes bore through me. "I just want to make sure you get home okay."

I nod again, licking my suddenly dry lips. He makes me so nervous, and I'm not sure why. Despite our failed marriage, Cole was my best friend growing up. I never felt uncomfortable around him.

Until now. *That I can remember.*

"I don't want a repeat of what happened. I'll do anything to keep you safe."

My heart pounds. His voice, his tone, the way he's so close—it's so much to deal with. *Too* much.

I place my hand on his chest. "I'm so sorry, Cole. I wish I could flip a switch and make my memory come back. I'm so confused, and I just want to know what happened, but I can't force it."

"I know." He presses his forehead to mine.

It would be so easy to melt into his arms, to feel the security I know he brings. But being with him still scares me.

"Go inside. I'll see you tomorrow night." He lets out a sigh. "Give Kaia a hug and kiss for me."

"I will," I whisper.

"Good night, Brooke."

I turn, slide my key into the lock, and twist the door handle. Why does it feel so wrong to leave him on the other side of the door from me?

*Because you love him even though he broke your heart.*

*Because he's Kaia's father.*

*Because somehow you know he's telling the truth.*

For a moment, I stand, pressing my hand against the door.

"Brooke?"

I turn at the sound of Rosalyn's voice. Her eyebrows knit as she gives me a concerned look. "Hi, Rosalyn."

"Are you okay?"

I shrug. "Cole walked me home."

The concern melts from her face, and she smiles. "How is he?"

"About as confused as I am."

She walks toward me, and wraps her arms around my shoulders. "You two will work it all out. It's just going to take some time."

"I hope you're right." I sigh. "I feel like I'm letting Kaia and Cole down."

She shakes her head. "They both love you. And Cole knows you're still recovering. Like I said, it will all take time. Be patient."

I take a step back. "Thank you. I don't know what I'd do without you."

Smiling, Rosalyn takes my hands in hers. "You're like a daughter to me, Brooke. And your little one might as well be my granddaughter."

I laugh. "That's so true."

"I should get going. Good night."

Seconds later, the door clicks shut and I'm alone. Sitting on the couch, I bury my face in my hands. What a mess. It doesn't matter what I do, I end up hurting someone. And I'm hurting too.

I walk to the bedroom, open a drawer to find a nightgown, and pull out a large, gray T-shirt I don't recognize. When Cole dropped me home from hospital he said some of his things were here, and I guess this must be one of them. I drop it back in the drawer, pausing before picking it up again.

It smells fresh, washed with the same powder as my own clothes, and I'm a little disappointed it doesn't smell of him.

But it wouldn't hurt for me to wear it.

I strip off, and pull the shirt over my head. Taking a deep breath, I look at myself in the mirror. *Please remember.*

Shaking my head, I climb into bed and pull the blankets over me.

I stare at the ceiling until my eyes grow heavy. Memories from long ago resurface, but not the ones I want.

*"I'm pregnant." I can barely look him in the eye, but I see enough of his pained expression to know this is the last thing he wants.*

*"What? How?" He waves his hands around. "That's not what I meant. We used a condom."*

*"Well, clearly it didn't work." I reach for his hand, but he tugs it away.*

*"Is it mine?"*

*My mouth falls open. "You know it is."*

*He sighs. "I do. Sorry." He takes my hand. "It's a shock."*

*"For me too."*

*He licks his lips. "So, what do we do? How do we take care of this?"*

*I stare at him. Tears prick my eyes despite my vow not*

to cry. "Take care of it? Are you telling me you want me to get rid of our baby?"

The look of horror on his face tells me that's not what he was thinking. I shouldn't jump to conclusions, but it's hard not to when it feels like the world's already against us.

"No. God, Brooke. This fucks everything up, but I would never suggest that. All the plans we made are out the window, so forgive me if I'm not saying the right thing right now." He takes me in his arms, but it feels forced. Like he's making himself do it. "Dad is going to kill me."

I sniff. "My mom is going to kill me."

"You know my dad is going to think this whole thing was some kind of plot by your mother to get cash from him."

I nod.

"He'll never accept that it was just an accident," I whisper.

Cole shakes his head and grips my chin, raising my gaze to his. "Our baby's not an accident. It must just have been meant to be."

"Mommy?"

Kaia. She walks into my room, a sweet smile on her face.

"Hey, baby. I thought you were asleep." I roll over as she climbs into bed beside me.

She snuggles in my arms. "I miss Daddy."

Swallowing down the tears that are forming, I hold her tight. "I know you do. I'm sorry."

"Did I do something wrong?"

My heart hurts. "No, baby."

"Why doesn't he come and visit? He can sleep in my bed."

I take a deep breath in her hair. "Mommy's still not completely better from her accident."

"Oh. Can Daddy come when you're better?"

I'm glad for the dark when tears roll down my cheeks. Kaia doesn't need to see me upset. "I'm sure he can. Maybe he can visit soon."

"I hope so. I miss him."

Within minutes she's fast sleep, and I plant a kiss on the top of her head before rolling onto my back.

I close my eyes.

Sleep will be slow to come. I already know that.

In the dark, I can only come to one conclusion.

I miss Cole too.

**3**

———

BROOKE

I RUB my neck and sigh.

The alarm blares in my ear and I'm so tired, but I have to get up.

I have to focus on my routine.

After two weeks off work, I went back to my day job. The following week, I started back at the night job. I'm exhausted.

I blink rapidly at the bright bathroom light when I enter the room. It's way too early in the morning for me to deal with getting up, but I have to. This is my life.

There are bags under my eyes that have been growing these past couple of weeks. I'm getting as much sleep as I can, but it never seems to be enough.

I open the drawer and pick up my hairbrush. My eyes fall upon the packet of tampons in the drawer. When was the last time I needed one?

The accident was six weeks ago.

My heart thuds. I've been so pre-occupied with everything else, I haven't noticed my missed period. That's only ever happened one time before. I'm as regular as clockwork.

*No. It's just some weird after-effect of the surgery or something.*

*No. I can't be.*

It doesn't matter how I try to reassure myself, it doesn't work. It would explain the extent of my exhaustion.

*Shit.*

Kaia sits up when I walk back into the bedroom.

"Can we see Daddy today?"

I shrug. "I'm not sure, baby. How about I talk to him and we sort something out?" Smiling, I reach for her hand. "Let's go and get some breakfast."

She's distracted by her cornflakes while I slowly sip my coffee. The thought of getting dressed and going to work is overwhelming, but sitting at home doesn't pay the bills.

*How would I deal with another baby?*

Kaia and I have just reached the point where we manage our routine. The early days after Cole left were the worst. While I had my mother, I still worked during the day despite all the sleepless nights.

Thankfully, when Kaia turned one she decided she liked her sleep. That was when I felt almost on top of things. We had no money, but we had each other.

*Can I rely on Cole?*

That's the million-dollar question.

---

I STOP at the pharmacy on the way to work and buy a pregnancy test. To be sure, I buy a two pack.

My mind can't process this. I know I was back in a relationship with Cole before I lost my memory, but my head is telling me that I haven't had sex since way before then. If I'm pregnant, it feels like it's been an immaculate conception.

Feeling that way creates a disconnect I'm not sure I can bridge any time soon. Before the accident is a blur, but buried in there somewhere is the possible creation of another child.

I wish more than anything that I could remember. What we felt on the night of Kaia's conception was always what held me together when times were tough. That Kaia was born out of love.

Even if that love only lasted a short time.

"Good morning." Jenny smiles as I take my seat at reception. I almost feel like I should hold my fingers up to form a cross sign to ward her off. She's so un-Jenny-like.

"Morning."

"How are you doing today?"

I nod. "Good. Tired, but good."

"Not too tired I hope."

Ugh. She's being too nice. It's like *Invasion of the Body Snatchers.* "Just settling back into the old routine."

"Let me know if you need anything."

I smile. "Thank you."

She disappears into her office, and I breathe a sigh of relief. This is what the past month's been like. I think she got a real fright over what happened to me.

I look down at my bag.

*Let's get this over with.*

I duck into the bathroom.

There's no way I'm waiting to check this. If it's negative, at least I'll be put out of my misery and I can speak to the doctor about my missing period next time I see him.

It's the longest two minutes of my life.

There are two pink lines.

TWO pink lines.

I pull out the spare test and pee on that too.

Two minutes. Two more lines.

*I'm pregnant.*

Son-of-a-bitch.

It's been six weeks since the accident, and I'm two weeks overdue. I don't remember getting my period in hospital either, but given the shock at my near-death experience, I'm not that surprised.

I'm not sure whether to be happy, sad, or angry at Cole. Even if it's half my fault. He left me last time we had a baby. Will he take responsibility for this one?

I clean up and make my way to reception, the two positive tests in my bag. I'm not sure what to do, but my mind sure as hell isn't on work.

"Are you okay?" Jenny asks as I return to the desk.

I nod. "Do you mind if I take a longer lunch break today? I have something I need to take care of."

She shakes her head. "That's no problem at all. Need help with anything?"

"I don't think so. I've also got my neurologist to see next week too."

"That's fine."

I don't want to take her change in attitude for granted, and I appreciate a little leeway. Especially as I get my life back on track.

Although this morning's discovery is going to set it all off-kilter again.

"Thank you. I really appreciate it. I'll miss my afternoon break to make up for it."

"You don't have to do that."

"Thank you."

As she walks away, I let out a long breath. Cole needs to know. It's only right he's the first person I tell. He told me he works not that far from here, so

I'll just go and get it over with.

And hope he doesn't abandon me again.

───────

IT'S A SUNNY DAY, and although there's a chill in the air, it's lovely and warm in the sun.

I walk to Cole's work, the news playing over and over in my head. *How the hell do I tell him?*

It doesn't help that I keep thinking about the way he reacted the first time. I can't get past that.

But I have to do it.

I walk across the car park toward the building.

As I reach the entrance, a tall, blond man walks out and does a double take.

"Brooke." The man smiles widely, and I cock an eyebrow. *Who is this?* "I'm Mike. A friend of Cole's. It's good to see you looking so well." He holds out his hand, and I shake it.

"Thanks. It's good to feel so well."

"You gave us quite a fright. Well, not you. I hope they catch the bastard who attacked you."

"Me too."

"I'll show you the way to Cole's office. I'm assuming you're here to see him."

"Yes." I nod.

"Cole's so proud of you and Kaia. I hear about you two all the time."

My cheeks burn. I love that Cole's told people

about us, but at the same time what exactly has he told them?

"This way." Mike leads me through the busy reception of the office building and down a corridor leading to a row of offices.

Turning toward the end, we walk into a room. There's a woman sitting at a desk who gives me a curious look.

"Brooke, this is Liz. She's Cole's PA. Liz, this is Brooke."

The woman gives me a strained smile. "*The* Brooke? It's so good to meet you."

For some reason, my guard goes straight up. I doubt that she doesn't like me. She doesn't seem know me, but her expression is hard to read.

"I thought I'd pop in and see Cole if he's not busy."

She nods. "I'm sure he's not too busy for you. Take a seat and I'll let him know you're here."

Mike guides me to a large, leather couch against the wall.

I sit, and smile at him. "Thank you."

The door opens, and Cole walks out.

"Brooke?" His eyes light up, and it dawns on me that coming here has given him hope. I can't bear to see it. It's one of the reasons I've been avoiding him. "This is a nice surprise. You didn't let me know you were coming."

I burst into tears despite my promise to myself to

be strong. My head's been in such a spin, I didn't even think to contact him first. Liz stares at me like I've got two heads, and Mike backs away.

"Come here." Cole slips one arm around my shoulder as I stand, and leads me into his office to an equally large couch. I sit as he closes the door behind us and sits with me.

"Hey." He pulls me into his arms, and I lean my head against his. "What's going on?"

I can't even find the words, and I reach into my bag and pull out the white stick. The one that keeps reminding me that we've done it again.

Without any words, I hand it to him.

He lets go of me and takes it. My stomach plummets at the shocked expression on his face. His initial reaction when I told him I was pregnant with Kaia terrified me. This is no different.

Until his lips curl into a smile.

"What? How?"

"Do I need to explain to you how babies are made, Cole?" I try my best to bring levity to the situation.

He chuckles. "No, but why wasn't this picked up earlier? The doctors have been all over you with tests, haven't they?"

I shrug. "I guess they weren't looking for pregnancy. And it must have been really early when I was in hospital. My period was due about then. I guess I've missed two."

He hugs me tighter.

"So, what do we do now?" I ask.

"I'm not sure. What do you want to do?" His lips are against my ear, and I close my eyes. Already the butterflies that were in my stomach are calming, even though nothing has been resolved.

"I don't know either." I lick my lips. "I've been avoiding dealing with us because I don't know how to. There's no way to keep doing that. We have to make some decisions together."

He breaks away from me and nods. "I want you and Kaia to move in with me. And as painful as it is, I know you don't want to do that. But I want you to know that no matter what, I'm here to do whatever you need me to. Financially and emotionally."

Tears prick my eyes. This is so much better than the conversation we had when I discovered I was pregnant with Kaia. Cole was supportive then, but there's something different now.

"I won't run, Brooke. I'm here for the long haul. Because I love you so much."

I let out a loud breath as the tears roll down my cheeks. It hurts that I can't tell him I love him in return because my emotions are a jumble of what happened in the past, and fragments of memory that are too hard to reach.

He links his fingers with mine. "I know you don't feel the same way right now, but you did, and I know some day you will again. I'll wait. I have four bedrooms in my house, so me asking you to move in with me doesn't mean I'm assuming you'll sleep with me."

"There's so much to think of. If we do that, it's a lot harder to get to my night job."

"You'd still do that?

I bite the inside of my cheek. "I need security, Cole. I need to know that if you're not around, I can pay my bills."

"I'm not going anywhere. Even if you don't move in, I'll make sure you have enough money to stay home with Kaia in the evenings. I don't want you back at that place. You should be safe to walk home, but I can't trust that you will be."

"And I can't trust that you're going to stay and keep giving me child support. Look at what happened before."

There's so much pain in his eyes, but I'm not responsible for that. He made his choice, and it nearly killed me.

"Things are different now. We were strong and in love. And we have another baby on the way. I'm not going anywhere."

"I just wish I felt that."

The last thing I want to do is hurt him, but I do. It's written all over his face.

I leave his office as confused as I was when I arrived.

It's time to go back to work.

# 4

### COLE

*Five years ago*

I WIPE the sweat from my brow with the back of my hand. It stings my eyes, and I blink to try and get rid of it.

"Want a towel?" Brooke asks. "I can go and ask your mother for one."

"No, I'm fine. I've just got to change the spark plugs now and I'm done." I smile. "This must be boring for you."

She chews on her bottom lip. I know that look.

"What are you thinking about?"

She shrugs. "I was wondering if you wanted to go to the prom with me."

For a moment, there's an awkward silence. Her cheeks flush with color, and she looks away.

"Okay, I guess not."

I shake my head. "Brooke, it's not that I don't want to. I already asked Kelly."

"Kelly Peterson?"

"Yeah." I suck in a breath because I know there's no love lost between Brooke and Kelly. Kelly's got a lot of bitchy friends, and none of them make time for Brooke.

"Good luck with that." Brooke looks down at her feet.

"I didn't think you'd be going to the prom. You never go out to any other social events."

"My mom saved and got me a dress."

My stomach falls to my knees. Brooke's mom is all she has, and the woman spends half her life drunk. For her to get herself together enough to do that for her daughter says a lot about how much the prom means to her.

"That's awesome." I lick my lips. "I'm really sorry. A week ago, things might have been different."

She shrugs. "It's okay. I should get going. I've got to cook dinner tonight. Mom's working."

"Do you want to have dinner here?"

She shakes her head. "No. It's fine. See you on Monday."

"Let me give you a lift home."

"I've got my bike. See you later."

I watch as she climbs onto her bike and cycles down my driveway. I'm never sure how to help her. She's the best friend I've ever had, and I want to do more for her, but I just know what my father would say.

As if summoned, he appears in the doorway leading into the house.

I close the hood of the car, and pick up the toolbox to put it away.

"Cole."

I turn to see Dad approach.

"What was Brooke doing here?"

"She's my friend, Dad. We were just hanging out."

He frowns. "You need to discourage her. I know you two are close, but she's not the type of girl you want around."

My anger grows. "What type is that?"

"Her mother doesn't exactly have a sterling reputation."

"She's not responsible for her mother's actions."

"Maybe not, but that girl is tarred with the same brush. Believe me. She's hung around long enough. Cut the string before she puts her hand out."

I drop the toolbox to the ground. It hits hard, the tools inside clanging together as they smack into each other.

"She's never once asked for anything. She's not like that. Maybe if you took the time to get to know her—"

"I don't need to. I watched her mother suck her father dry until he died."

"That doesn't mean Brooke will be anything like her. She has a job, Dad, and she doesn't want anything from me. We're friends."

He runs his fingers through his graying hair. "Just be careful."

"Of what?

He turns and walks away. It makes me so angry. Mom has always been the one to welcome Brooke with open arms, but as we've gotten older, Dad's been pushing me to drop her as a friend.

I'll never do that.

I pinky promised.

---

THE PROM'S the following month.

Fleming Reid asked Brooke to go with him, and she accepted, and it bugs me because I've heard the way he's talked about his sexual conquests. Other than that, he's not a bad guy. I've known him nearly as long as I've known Brooke. I guess I just don't want to see my best friend hurt.

I slip my arm around Kelly's shoulders as we walk toward the school hall and take a deep breath.

"I've been looking forward to this for weeks," she purrs, placing her hand on my chest.

Rock music pours out of the building, and we

reach the door where teachers nod in recognition as we pass.

This is it. We're all so close to leaving school and going onto college. I can't wait. It means moving away from our small town, but I'm ready for it. I'm ready for anything.

"Cole." Fleming smiles as we approach.

I fist bump him, and he grins.

"Hey," he says.

"Hey, Fleming."

"Ready for a big night?"

I nod. "It's so good not to have exam stress."

"Tell me about it."

Gina Roberts walks toward us, a glass of punch in each hand. "Here we go." She hands the second glass off to Fleming, and an uneasy feeling crawls over me.

"I thought you were here with Brooke Stevens."

He shakes his head. "Nope."

"She told me you asked her."

Gina laughs. "Whatever. As if Fleming would have anything to do with that trash."

Anger builds in me. "Don't talk about her like that. She's not a liar."

She points at her shimmering gold gown. "This cost three hundred dollars. What would she have worn anyway? Something from Walmart?"

"Cole." Kelly touches my arm, but I shake her off. "I'll go and get us a drink."

I don't even acknowledge her as I stare Fleming down.

"I'll go with Kelly. You two can talk." Gina rolls her eyes and disappears through the crowd.

"What the fuck, dude?" I ask as soon as the girls leave us.

Fleming shrugs. "I did ask her, but I got a better offer."

"A better offer?"

He grins the sleaziest grin I think I've ever seen. "Gina's good to go. Your girl wasn't going to put out."

A knot forms in my stomach. Brooke never said a word about this, but I do know how excited she was to be coming. She must have been devastated at the rejection. "What the hell is wrong with you?"

"Maybe you should worry more about your date, and less about someone who lives in that part of town. I don't know why you hang out with her. She's so—"

"So, what?" Heat and anger rise inside me. It spills out as I fist my hands. I know that Brooke is looked down upon by some of my classmates. She's smarter than all of them. And I'm not going to put up with them trashing her.

"Boring. Although maybe once someone gets some alcohol into that punch, it might make her more exciting. If you know what I mean." He winks, and it's the biggest mistake he ever could have made.

There's a crunch as my knuckles makes contact with his jaw. He goes down in a heap. Around us, people gasp. We've drawn a crowd.

Kelly comes racing back to my side, her eyes wide. "What did you do?"

"You're an asshole, you know that?" Fleming says, rubbing his jaw.

"Maybe you should look in the mirror when you say that." My hands are still fisted. My fury knows no bounds. His disrespect of my best friend is the end of whatever friendship I thought we had.

"What's your problem?"

Two large hands appear on my shoulders, and I'm tugged backward. I find myself looking at Coach Belkin and his assistant.

"Out, Masters," Coach says.

"You can't kick him out," Kelly cries.

"We told you all that there'd be no tolerance for this kind of thing."

I nod. There's no point causing further trouble. I meet Kelly's wild gaze. She's pissed, and I can't blame her. But there's also no way I'm apologizing for this.

It's like everything makes sense. I thought that Brooke had won some of our classmates over with her sweet, gentle manner. Instead, these people are just a bunch of snobs. Snobs who don't deserve her.

"How am I supposed to get home?" Kelly asks.

I shove my hand in my pocket and pull out my

wallet. There's always an emergency fifty-dollar note in there; my dad insists on it. I hand it to her. "This'll pay for a cab. Unless you want to come with me now."

She shakes her head. "I'm not leaving my prom because you were an idiot."

"Didn't think so."

Coach still has a grip on my shoulder. He squeezes it.

"You don't have to throw me out. I'll leave."

He releases me, and I walk away from the music and the other people I thought were friends. Brooke's always been special to me. She's helped keep me grounded. I thought we were all old enough to be over that.

For a moment, I sit in my car and stew. How dare Fleming assume that Brooke would sleep with him after a few drinks? Anger surges inside me again, and I just want to go back and have another go.

And what about Brooke? Why didn't she tell me what Fleming did? Or let me know she wasn't going to be at the prom?

It breaks my heart thinking someone could hurt my best friend like this. Is this how a best friend's supposed to feel, or am I feeling more? I love Brooke, but am I *in* love with her?

I drive to Brooke's house. She needs me. Running from my car, I hammer on her door. Brooke's mother opens it.

"Cole?"

"Is Brooke home?"

"Brooke's at the prom." She slurs her words. Clearly she's been drinking already.

"She's not here?"

"She left a while ago. I don't know if I like the boy she went with. She got a cab. He should have picked her up."

I nod. "Yeah, he should have. Have a good night, Mrs. Stevens."

She smiles. "It's a shame you two didn't go together. You'd make such a lovely couple."

As if I don't already regret taking Brooke up on her offer. *You could have asked her instead of Kelly, you idiot.*

The truth is that it never occurred to me. I spend a lot of time with Brooke, and we usually confide in each other. She didn't tell me anything about Fleming other than he'd asked her to the prom.

For a moment, I sit in my car and rack my brain for any idea of where Brooke might be. *Somewhere far enough to need a cab.*

Maybe she's not that far at all.

Apart from my house, her favorite place in the world is the beach. The wind is chilly, and if that's where she's gone I hope she's somewhere where she's not too cold.

I drive to the beach. There's no one around, and I breathe a sigh of relief when I spot her.

She's in her prom dress sitting on a rock, looking out to sea. Her blond hair's piled on her head and set in place with some glittery hairpiece.

I've never seen her look so beautiful.

My chest twinges. Do I … do I have feelings for Brooke?

"Brooke," I call.

She looks up as I run toward her, her eyes a brilliant blue brought out by her royal blue gown.

"What are you doing here?" she asks.

"Looking for you. It's freezing."

She shrugs. "I like the fresh air." She drops her gaze. "How did you find me?"

"I know it's your favorite place." I smile. "There's a lot I know about you."

Slipping off the rock, she stands before me. "You know more about me than anyone. And I'll ask you again, what are you doing here? Shouldn't you be at prom with Kelly?"

"I got thrown out."

Her eyes widen. "Why?"

"Punching Fleming."

Brooke's mouth falls open.

"Why didn't you tell me how he treated you? He's a pig."

She looks down at her feet. "You don't need to hear my problems."

"That's what best friends are for."

When she looks back up at me, her eyes are full

of tears. "I didn't want to screw up your night. You should be able to go and enjoy it without worrying about me."

I grasp her chin, locking in her gaze so she can't pull away again. "Of course I worry about you. I wanted to do more than punch Fleming. I wanted to smack the shit out of him for the way he acted toward you."

"It's the way they always act toward me, Cole. Like they're better than me. At least next year they'll all be off to college and not around here anymore."

My skin prickles. "But you're going to college. You got a scholarship last semester."

She shakes free of my grasp. "I can't make it work. No matter what I do. It doesn't cover all my expenses and even if I get a part-time job, it'll just be too much."

"Shit." I lick my lips. "Maybe I can ask my dad to help."

"Cole, I'm not stupid. Your father hates me."

"He doesn't hate you."

"Well, he doesn't like me. And I know why. He thinks I'm like my mom."

"Has he said that to you?" *Bastard.*

She shakes her head. "I can see it in his face when he looks at me. I can't blame him. He blames Mom for the loss of his best friend."

"How do you know that?"

"She tells me stories when she's drunk. About

how, despite their differences, my dad was close with your dad." Brooke looks at me from under her lashes. "Friends like we are."

She shivers.

I slip my jacket from my shoulders and place it over hers. She looks up at me. "Thanks. Aren't you cold?"

I shrug. "I'll survive. What are you doing out here?"

"It seemed like a good place to spend the evening. It's quiet."

"No one to see you."

She fixes her gaze on me and nods. "I can't let my mother know she spent all this money on a dress just for me to not go."

"Why didn't you tell me you weren't going? I thought you were."

Brooke looks at her feet. "I was. But then it became clear that Fleming had … expectations."

I nod. "I know. He told me he ditched you because you wouldn't put out."

Her mouth drops open as she stares at me. "He didn't."

"He had Gina on his arm tonight."

She sighs. "He told me he'd booked a motel room for us. I freaked out. I've never dated the guy. Why would I sleep with him?"

"Prom tradition, apparently." I slip my arm

around her shoulders. "If you don't want to face your mom, come back to my house for a while."

"You know I can't."

"I'll sneak you into my room. Like we used to when we were kids."

She laughs. "We haven't done that in a long time."

"Tonight seems to be a night to break all the rules. What's another one?"

---

My room is right at the end of the house, and the balcony extends all the way. I'm thankful there's no window for Brooke to try and scramble through in that gown of hers. She can walk right in the sliding door, once I open it.

I push open the back door and walk through the kitchen and into the living room. Mom and Dad sit watching television, and Dad looks up at me in surprise. "What happened to your prom? Did you lose your jacket?"

"I got kicked out for punching Fleming Reid."

"Oh, Cole." Mom's eyes are so sad.

"What the hell, Cole? Why would you do that?" Dad says.

"He's a douche."

"What about your date?" Mom asks.

"I gave her money to get a taxi home. She wanted to stay."

"At least you did that. How disappointing." Dad gives me such a look of disdain that all the anger I felt before comes flooding back.

"Fleming was supposed to take Brooke. He dumped her for another girl because Brooke wouldn't sleep with him."

Mom's mouth falls open. "Poor Brooke."

"I wasn't about to let him treat my best friend like that. Brooke wanted to go so badly, and her mom …" My voice cracks. "Her mom paid for a dress she won't get to use. It's so unfair."

Dad nods. "That is unfair. Do you want me to speak to Fleming's father?"

I raise my eyebrows. Dad agreeing with me is the last thing I thought would happen. We butt heads a lot, but even he can see why I'm angry about this.

"I'm not sure if there's much point. You can do if you want to. I'm not sure how receptive he'll be, given I punched Fleming in the face."

The corners of Dad's mouth curl into a smile. "I'm glad you stood up for her. Especially if no one else was going to."

Mom pats Dad's arm, smiling at him.

"I'm going to go and watch a movie in my room. What a fucked up night."

"Cole," Mom snaps.

I laugh. "Sorry." I walk over to her, and press a kiss to her forehead while she cups my cheek.

"I'm so proud of you."

"Goodnight, Mom. Dad."

"Goodnight," Dad says.

I make my way to my room, tugging at my tie.

Brooke stands on the deck. Despite my jacket, she shivers, and after locking my door, I walk toward the deck. Unlocking it, I slide that door open and she slips in.

"You okay?" I ask.

"Just cold."

"It's warm in here. Is your mother going to notice if you're gone for the night?"

Her eyes widen.

"I'll take you home if you want. But if you stay, you can take the bed. I'll sleep on the floor."

She nods, dropping my jacket from her shoulders and handing it to me.

"I'm proud of you, you know?"

She laughs as she sits on the bed. "Why?"

"For not just letting Fleming have what he wants."

She grimaces. "I like him, but not enough to end up in a motel room with him. Besides, I've heard stories of his conquests. Why would I want stories spread about me?"

I throw my jacket over the back of my computer chair. "He's a prick. He'd talked about girls, but I didn't think he'd be like that with you."

She shakes her head. "I don't want my first time

to be with someone who thinks it'll be fun to tell the world."

My breathing quickens. Brooke and I have talked about everything in our lives, except sex. It was always an unspoken promise between us not to. But this doesn't feel uncomfortable.

"I always thought you had been with Justin. You dated him for six months."

She stares at me as if I've just sworn. "No. I mean, he wanted to, but I couldn't. Not with him."

"He worshipped the ground you walked on, B."

"I always thought it'd be you." She says it so quietly, I almost miss it. *What?*

"Thought it would be me?"

She stands. For a moment, we stare at each other.

"Brooke," I say softly.

Her expression tightens as she swallows, and she blinks a bunch of times as if she's fighting tears. "It's stupid. I know. Maybe I should go home."

My heart's in my throat. Maybe home is the right place for her to be, but I've got a yearning I've never had before and that's to hold her in my arms and never let her go.

I cross the room and palm her cheek. "I never knew you felt that way."

"Forget what I said." She pulls away.

"How can I?"

*I don't want you to go.*

*My heart's just woken up.*

*I love you.*

"I need to go home." She sucks in her top lip. "I'll call for a taxi. Stay here and enjoy your night."

She takes a step toward the sliding door.

"Don't go," I say.

"I've made enough of an idiot of myself tonight." She licks her lips and takes another step toward her escape route.

"Stay here with me." I step closer.

She does that rapid blinking thing again. "Cole, I feel stupid. Mom's probably asleep by now anyway."

"I'm not thinking about your mother." Her blue eyes widen as I stroke her cheek. Tears well in her eyes. "I've been so blind, Brooke. You've been right in front of me all along. I love you."

She licks her lips as tears escape her eyes and roll down her cheeks. "Not in *that* way."

"Maybe I do. Maybe I just didn't realize it." I sigh. "There was no way I was staying at the prom once I knew what had happened to you. All I wanted was to find you and make sure you were okay. Because I care about you. As more than just a friend."

"Cole Masters, if you're saying this to get laid …"

I shake my head. "I just want to kiss you."

Her chest rises sharply as she takes a deep breath. "You're not obligated to make me feel better about tonight."

"If you think this is about obligation, you're crazy."

She swallows so hard I see the movement in her throat. "Cole," she says softly.

Her face is so close to mine, and I study her features for a moment. I always knew she was pretty. God knows when we were kids, we were teased about being boyfriend and girlfriend, but we were only ever friends.

At least, that was what I thought.

Maybe it was always meant to be something more.

She nods, and I gently press my mouth to hers. Her lips are soft, and there's a hint of grape from her gloss.

When she parts her lips, I slip my tongue in and caress hers. There's the tiniest of gasps that comes from her throat.

"All this time and you were right there." Emotion overwhelms me.

"I thought you'd never see me."

"All I see is you." I kiss her again before leaning my forehead on hers. "Stay?"

"Okay."

# 5

COLE

Present day

SHE'S PREGNANT.

It doesn't change anything when it comes to my feelings about Brooke, but it does increase my need to unite our family.

I'm haunted by memories. Since Brooke's memory loss, I've been reliving pivotal moments of our lives.

*Brooke showing me her feelings.*

*The night Kaia was conceived.*

Things could have been so different for us. If I'd stayed, Brooke wouldn't have had her accident, and maybe if I'd held things together, we'd be happily married instead of in this big mess that exists now.

And now we have two children involved.

I lie awake in bed and think about Brooke and Kaia. We were a family for a short time again, and this time I can't see my way back to them.

Maybe I won Brooke over before, but with the added issues around her memory loss, she's doubled down on not trusting me. I understand it, but it doesn't make it hurt any less.

*My little girl laughing with delight when she laid eyes on her room.*

I get out of bed and walk down the hallway to Kaia's room. It was too painful to look at, and I shut the door on it weeks ago. Now, I open the door and walk in.

Flicking the button that lights the room with projected stars, I pick up the stickers I bought to decorate. Our movie night inspired me, and I have a huge selection of Pixar characters ready to stick on the wall.

I wanted to do this with Kaia.

It's a little after two in the morning as I open the first one and place it in the center of the wall. It's Dory. Kaia wanted to watch *Finding Nemo* twice after Brooke left for work. I had promised her we'd watch it again. We never got to do that.

One by one, the stickers go up until I've covered the wall. There's something for every movie we watched and some that are a promise of ones we haven't seen together.

*We'll watch them together, Kaia. Maybe with your new baby brother or sister.*

The sun is rising when I finish, the early morning rays peeping through the curtains. I'm no closer to finding a way to make Brooke trust me, but the wall is finished and ready for Kaia to see.

Now to shower and start getting ready for work.

---

I CAN BARELY KEEP my eyes open.

"Are we keeping you awake?" Mike stands in the doorway to my office. Everyone at work knows about the situation with Brooke, and they've been caring and understanding. It leaves me wondering how Brooke is doing with that bitchy boss. Is she being treated fairly too?

"I was up half the night decorating Kaia's room."

Mike smiles. "You should do that on the weekends, Cole. Then you wouldn't be struggling to stay awake at your desk."

"Inspiration struck. Besides, I got some news yesterday that left me not able to sleep."

"Is that why Brooke was here?"

I nod. Mike's been my friend and confidante for a year, and I need someone to talk to. "She's pregnant."

For a moment, he just blinks. "Wow. Who's the father?"

I glare at him. "Me. It must have happened right before the attack."

"Well, you two were at it like bunnies."

I laugh. "Not that you were ever told that."

He shrugs. "Come on. She's gorgeous, and you're a red-blooded male. You'd have to be crazy not to want to have a lot of sex with her."

"Can you please stop talking about my wife like that?" I laugh.

"At least you're smiling."

I lean back in my chair. "It's not easy. I just miss them so much."

"I told you before and I'll tell you again: patience. Pushing her is only going to backfire on you. She needs time."

"You've turned into a real counselor."

He smiles. "I just want to see you happy again. And not falling asleep at your desk."

I laugh. "I promise I'll get an early night tonight."

"Good luck."

I sigh as he leaves my office.

I'm going to need all the luck I can get.

**6**

---

BROOKE

I'm so glad I'm only working five nights a week and not six. I want to spend more time with Kaia, and I'm going to need all the rest I can get in the coming weeks.

My morning sickness with Kaia was awful. I don't know if it helped our marriage that Cole would sometimes hold my hair while I puked. He tried to be sweet, but that was pretty gross.

It's Sunday afternoon, and I'm so tired I'm almost asleep on the couch. I haven't heard from Cole, but I haven't reached out to him either since the other day. I'm still not sure what to think. He's saying all the right things, and I'm leaning toward trusting him. I did let him get close enough to impregnate me again, after all.

"Mommy, look." Kaia grins up at me from the

floor. She's been playing with her building blocks and used them all to make a big tower that's about to topple over.

I laugh. "It's nearly as tall as you."

She grins.

My heart leaps at the knock on the door, and I push myself off the couch.

"Who is it?" I ask as I approach.

"Jensen Masters."

I fist my hands without thinking about it. Never in a million years did I think Cole's father would be on my doorstep. But then again, he and Cole's mother were wonderful when I was in hospital.

He's kept his word and stayed away until now.

I'm grateful to him for making sure I didn't have hospital bills, but it was the least he could do considering the way he'd treated me.

I take a deep breath and pull open the door.

"Grandpa," Kaia squeals, launching herself off the floor. She runs straight at him, and he closes his eyes as she wraps her arms around his thighs.

"Hi, Kaia. I've got a gift for you." He meets my gaze. "I hope that's okay."

I nod. "It's fine."

We just look at each other for a moment before I wake myself out of my daze. "Sorry, come in."

He walks through the door, Kaia right beside him, and looks around the room. I hope he's happy. I hope he realizes us living here is his fault. He took our little house away from us.

"First of all, here you go." He hands Kaia a wrapped package, and she looks at me.

"It's okay, baby. You can open it now." I smile.

She drops to the floor in front of the couch. The paper flies as she tears it off, and my smile widens at how happy she is. "Thank you," I say.

"I wasn't sure if you'd let me in. But I'm in town on business, and I wanted to see how you were doing."

"Take a seat and I'll make coffee."

He nods, taking a seat on the couch.

While I spoon the coffee into the mugs, a million thoughts run through my head. Should I tell Cole's father about the baby? Has Cole already told him? Is that why he's here? I'm not sure if I'm ready for him to know yet.

When I step back into the living room, Jensen's eyes are fixed on Kaia. The joy in his expression is gratifying to see. Her life is what he missed out on, and that's on him.

"Need help with the box, baby girl?" I ask.

"No, Mommy." She grins up at me.

I hand Jensen his coffee and sit on the couch.

"I suppose you're wondering why I'm here." He takes a sip of his drink and places the cup on the coffee table.

I nod. "The hospital was rough, but I want you to know I appreciate everything you did for me."

"It's an open-ended offer. I'll take care of all your medical bills because we need you to be well." He sighs. "What I wanted to do was explain things to you. There's a lot you don't know about my connection to your family."

"I know you were friends with my father."

He gives me a wistful smile. "Your father meant the world to me. We were best friends when we started school. Much like you and Cole were."

I suck on my bottom lip and nod.

"I met Nicole in high school. And Joseph met your mother. We left school, got jobs, got married. Only your mother wasn't happy. Her father was an alcoholic, and she followed in his footsteps." He takes a deep breath. "Anyway, I discovered she was sleeping around. Joseph didn't believe me at first. Then she announced she was pregnant."

I swallow hard.

"No matter what, Joseph adored you. He vowed that whether you were his or not, he would love you and take care of you. And he did. But Dana just kept drinking." There are tears in his eyes. My father's death was sudden. He went to work one day, had a heart attack, and never came home. I never thought about Cole's father losing his friend.

"He worked so hard. I miss him every day," I say.

"So do I. Your mother didn't want anything to do

with us after that. I was always surprised she didn't mind your friendship with Cole."

I shook my head. "She didn't seem to care about much. Not until Kaia came along. That's why I spent so much time at your house when I was growing up."

"I should have understood that better. For so long, I blamed her for my best friend's death. And you." He places his hand over mine. "I should never have blamed you. You were a child. And then you became pregnant and said it was my son's. I didn't know if I was watching Dana all over again, but I didn't want Cole to end up like Joseph."

Tears roll down my cheeks. "You were so awful to us."

"I know, and I'm sorry. Here you are working yourself to the bone to provide for you and your daughter. I should never have done what I did. Even if Kaia wasn't Cole's, I should have taken better care of you. Joseph would have wanted it."

"It's taken you a long time to work that out. There was never any doubt that Kaia was Cole's. He's her father."

He nods. "When Cole called and said you were in hospital, all I could think about was Joseph. That's why I came. And the second I laid eyes on Kaia, I knew I'd been wrong. She's you and Cole through and through." He lets out a loud breath. "I'm so sorry, Brooke. I hope you can forgive me."

"Mommy, look."

I turn my head to look at Kaia. A couple of weeks ago, she saw a toy on TV she told me she desperately wanted. It was a dog that moved and barked and talked. And it was way out of my budget.

Now she holds one in her arms.

"Let me fix that for you." Some of the ties haven't come off, and it's still attached to the box. I untwist them, freeing the toy. "Oh, baby. He's beautiful."

"He's my friend." She hugs him tight.

I swallow. "Say thank you to Grandpa."

"Thank you, Grandpa." She launches herself at the couch, wedging herself between Cole's father and me.

"You're very welcome. You were so excited when we saw the ad on TV for it when we were staying in the hotel."

She beams. I watch his face as he watches her. There's a strain there, and I can see the emotions he's feeling as he takes in her excitement. There's love and regret—something I never thought I'd see from him.

As she plays, he moves his gaze to me. "Joseph would be so proud of you. I'm so sorry he never lived to see Kaia."

I nod. "Me too. I miss him so much."

"He loved you with everything he had. And Cole loves you just as much."

I wipe my cheeks with the back of my hand. "I wish I could remember."

"I know you do." His eyes are warm, and I see an affection in them I never saw before. "I can't tell you how sorry I am. It wasn't just seeing Kaia that shook me—it was seeing you in that hospital bed. I've been haunted by it ever since, and thinking of Joseph since that day."

"I was always so scared you'd try and take Kaia from me."

He shakes his head. "Never. Even if I had believed the worst, she needs you. But I think she also needs Cole now she knows him. I'm not asking for another chance for me, Brooke, but I'd really appreciate you giving Cole one."

I lick my lips, and run my fingers through Kaia's curls. "I've been thinking about him a lot."

"Being apart from you two is killing him. And Nicole is itching to see Kaia. She doesn't know I'm here, but she'd love to spend time with both of you."

I nod. "I'd love to see her. She was always so good to me."

"I know I wasn't."

"You wanted to protect Cole. I understand that much."

"Grandpa, look." Kaia puts her new toy on the floor. The dog walks, then barks, and asks for someone to play with him.

"I'm glad you like him."

"I love him." She picks the dog up and hugs him. "I wish we could get a real dog."

"We can't have pets here, Kaia, but one day." I give her a smile. I look back at Cole's father. "Thank you for coming. And for everything you've said. It means a lot."

"I'm glad I came. Seeing Cole so desperate hit me so hard. And then I thought about how hard things have been for you. It's all my fault."

I don't have anything else to say, so I shift my gaze back to Kaia. "How about we invite Daddy for dinner one night?"

Her eyes widen. "Can we?"

"Sure. Maybe we can have some pizza."

"Pizza's my favorite. Daddy likes it too," she tells Jensen.

"Is it? I think your dad has good taste."

"Would you like to stay for dinner?" I ask.

"I'd love to. I'll pay."

While the past four years can't be erased, I know this is a huge step for a very proud man. He hasn't treated me well, but everything he's said means a lot. That he's prepared to swallow his pride and apologize says a lot.

He hands me some cash out of his wallet, and I pick up the phone to order pizza.

Seeing him get down onto the living room floor with Kaia to play with her toy fills my heart with joy. I can't forget what he did, nor can I forgive him, but I think we can move forward. Kaia's delighted with his presence, and I understand.

She has such a big heart, and he's her grandfather.

I order Kaia's favorite, pepperoni, and sit back and watch them play. Jensen is a changed man. He's all smiles, and that look of enchantment on his face while watching Kaia gives me a warm feeling.

She's the one who matters most in all of this. If she wants a relationship with her grandparents, then she'll have one. I won't stand in her way.

The time passes as I'm lost in thought, and the knock catches me by surprise.

"Brooke?" Jensen says.

"That'll be the pizza. Sorry. I was a million miles away."

I walk to the door and pull it open, inhaling the scent of oregano as I hand over the money and take the delivery.

"I'll get plates. Just point me in the right direction," Jensen says.

"Let's just put it on the table and eat there."

He grins. "I haven't done that in years."

I place the pizza down and open the boxes. My stomach grumbles at the smell of cheese and pepperoni.

"Pizza!" Kaia drops her dog on the floor and runs to the table.

I shake my head at her. "Your poor toy."

She shrugs and picks up a slice of pizza.

Jensen laughs. "That's nearly as big as your head."

Kaia grins, and takes a large bite. "Yummy."

"Is it, sweetheart? I'll have to try," he says.

I laugh. "I never saw you as a pizza man."

"I've never really been much of one. But if Kaia likes it, it must be good."

My heart's warmed by his enthusiasm for my daughter.

"She has good taste. This is the best pizza around here," I say.

Watching Jensen Masters eat pizza has to be one of the funniest things I've ever seen. Not because he does it in a weird way or anything, but because he was always a sit-at-the-table-and-use-the-silverware kind of person. I keep my thoughts to myself and enjoy the treat he's paid for.

Kaia plays up to him, fluttering her eyelashes and chatting away about anything and everything. Seeing her like this warms my heart. My life has been so chaotic, I never stopped to think about how lonely it was, for me and for her.

She loves having her grandfather in her life.

"Kaia, it's time for bed," I say after an hour.

She pouts.

Jensen taps her on the nose. "Listen to your mother. I'll come and see you again soon."

"Good night, Grandpa."

He pulls her onto his lap, and she wraps her arms around his neck.

"Good night, Kaia. Grandma and I love you."

"I love you too."

Hearing her so affectionate toward him tears at my heart.

Kaia takes my hand, and I lead her to her room where her pajamas wait. She wraps her arms around my neck as I button up the top.

"Can we see Daddy soon?" Kaia asks.

I smile. "Soon. Are you going to go straight to sleep?"

She nods.

I hug her tight, kissing her on the forehead, and lift her into her bed. She closes her eyes, and I sit with her for a few minutes, stroking her hair.

I place my other hand on my stomach. This child deserves to know its father. Just as Kaia did. She missed out on so much, but I'll be damned if she'll miss out on more. There's so much to work through in my head, but I need to do it for the sake of my children.

*Our* children.

For a moment, I sit and listen to her breathe. Kaia and I have been through a lot together. After Mom died, we moved four times before I found my job and we moved here. This has been her home longer than anywhere else. Her stability is so important.

She sighs, and I lean over and kiss her temple.

I swear I've never seen anyone fall asleep as fast

as she does, and I smile to myself as I stand and pull away.

Jensen looks up at me as I enter the room.

"Kaia asleep?" He smiles.

I nod. "Out like a light. It doesn't take much with her."

"She's so sweet. You've done such a great job raising her."

"Thank you." I sit on the couch. "Would you and Nicole like to see her more often?"

His eyes light up. "We'd love to."

"I'm not really in a position to travel a lot to see you, but I want you to know that you're more than welcome to come and visit us. Just let me know ahead of time so I can plan for it."

He nods. "Of course. Thank you. This will mean the world to Nicole." His eyebrows dip. "Things aren't that good between us right now. I lied to her, and that meant she missed out on Kaia too."

"I hope you can work things out."

"Me too. All I wanted was to protect my family, but I did the opposite. Anyway, I'm in town for a couple more days. Do you want to go out for dinner tomorrow night? My treat."

"I'm working."

He frowns. "I thought that you would have given that up. Is Cole giving you enough?"

I nod. "He's giving me plenty, but—"

"You don't want to give up that security yet."

"No. I can't." I let out a loud breath. "I'm sure both you and Cole mean what you're saying, but it's all just words right now. I need time to work out what to do. And I need to make sure that Kaia and I are secure before I give up that income."

He nods. "I understand. I'm not sure I like it, but I understand."

"You didn't seem to care before." The words come out without me thinking, but I have no regret.

"I'm ashamed of my behavior, but I did always know where you were."

"Did Cole know?"

He swallows hard. "No, and my actions have put a wedge between us that I regret. I hope in time he'll give me another chance."

I nod. "He loves you. I'm sure he will."

"He loves you. I've never heard him so angry as he was when he called me to confront me over the money. And I've never seen him fall apart the way he did when you were in the hospital."

Cole was angry about him withholding money from me. He didn't know. *Did I know this before the accident?* Maybe that's one of the reasons why I let him back in.

I swallow down tears. "You don't have to convince me. I know how he feels."

He smiles, and it's genuine, and that just makes me want to cry even more. Why couldn't he have been like this from the start?

"I'll get going. But I want you to call me if you or Kaia need anything. Anything at all."

I nod. "I will."

He stands, and I follow suit. "When I get home, I'll talk to Nicole. We'll come back together next time."

"That's fine. Kaia will love it." I screw up my face. "Can you please not bring her gifts every time, though?"

Jensen chuckles. "Of course. I just remembered how excited she was when she saw that ad for it, and when I spotted it in the store, it had Kaia written all over it."

"I don't want to sound ungrateful. But I don't want her taking it for granted."

"I understand." He bends to place a kiss on my cheek. "See you next time. I'll give you a call when we work out when we can be back."

"Sounds good."

When he leaves, I'm still not sure how I feel about Cole's father having anything to do with Kaia. He denied her parentage, denied her getting the support she should have had. But if my recovery from surgery has taught me anything, it's that life's so short.

Whatever my relationship with Jensen, Kaia deserves to get to know her grandparents. They're the only ones she has.

And Cole. Cole deserves better. I've been so torn

over him, but this little insight into what happened before the accident has helped. Maybe I need to open my heart to him again.

I'm not sure what the future will bring for me and my children, but our world is changing, whether I'm up with the play or not.

I just hope I'm ready.

**7**

---

BROOKE

MONDAY NIGHT at the bar is hard.

We have a rush from eight to ten, but it dies off by eleven. I'm grateful for the peace, and looking forward to going home. Fatigue is hard enough to fight without the late nights, but this is what I signed up for.

"Go home now if you want."

My eyebrows rise as I stare at Marcus. He's been as accommodating as Jenny has since the accident, but he never usually lets any of us go home early unless it is an emergency.

He smiles. "I'll pay you for the last hour. Go and be with your family."

"Thank you."

His expression softens. "We all nearly lost you, Brooke. I've never had something like that happen to someone so close. It scared the shit out of me."

"It still scares me. I wish I could remember what happened."

He nods. "I'm sure. Are you okay getting home?"

"I'm sure I'll be fine."

I have to face this if I'm going to get through. For a year, I walked home without incident, and I'm not letting this beat me.

Grabbing my bag, I say goodbye to Katie and Eric in the kitchen and head out toward the door.

"Brooke. You leaving early?" Craig looks up from the bar.

"I'm heading home. Have a good night."

He smiles. "You too. Is Cole coming to get you?"

I shake my head. "I'll be fine."

"Just be careful." His eyes convey his concern, and I'm grateful, but I need to take control of my life.

I walk out of the door and cross the street. Every step of the way, I'm watching where I'm going and looking all around me. My confidence is waning.

When I reach the end of the block, I freeze.

This is where it happened.

I walk past here by myself on the way to work every day. Now my head spins, and I feel faint. *Why can't I remember?*

Fear curls around my chest and pulls it tight.

A car drives slowly through the intersection. I can't make my feet move. It's like I'm stuck to the spot.

I look around. Apart from the car that just

passed, there doesn't seem to be anyone out here, but that doesn't help.

My eyes prick with tears.

*Cole. I need Cole.*

It's instinctive. I pull my phone out of my bag and dial. He answers straight away.

"Brooke?"

"Marcus let me go home early, and I'm halfway home. But I'm stuck. I can't move. I'm where it happened, and I'm frozen in place."

"I'll get in the car and come to you."

Tears stream down my cheeks. "This is so stupid."

"Not at all, sweetheart. Maybe it's a sign your memory's coming back?"

"I'm not sure."

"I'll be there really soon."

"Can you stay on the line with me?"

In the background, I hear the car door close. "Of course I can. Give me a second. This might cut out when I switch it to Bluetooth, but if it does, I'll call you right back."

"Okay," I whisper.

I palm my forehead. How embarrassing. I know Cole won't tease me, not about this, but I'm a grown woman who can't move from the spot she's in.

The car starts up. "On my way."

"Don't rush. I don't want you having an accident."

My head pounds. I'm not sure if it's stress or not, but my brain feels like it's expanding in my head.

"Remember when we were sixteen, and your mother grounded you for sneaking out of the house so I helped you out your window, and we spent the night on the beach?" Cole asks.

I smile, letting out a small laugh. "We were trouble."

"Yeah, we were. I should have known then we were destined to be together for life."

"Bonded in rebellion." *For life?* Is that how long we'll be together?

"Something like that." He pauses. "Are you okay?"

"Talking's helping."

"I'm not too far away. How was work?"

I lick my lips. "Busy. But it died off really quickly, so Marcus sent me home early."

"That doesn't sound like him, from what you've told me."

I laugh. "It's not. But I think what happened to me gave him a fright."

"He's not the only one."

Talking to Cole makes me less self-conscious. Butterflies take off in my stomach at the anticipation of seeing him. *I want his arms around me.*

He keeps me talking, and the time passes quickly.

I gasp when a hand touches my shoulder.

"Brooke, you okay? I'm nearly there," Cole says.

Turning, my eyes widen as John staggers toward me.

"What are you doing out here? You should be home." John slurs his words, and lifts his hand.

"My husband's coming to get me." My heart pounds.

He smiles. "Good. Don't want to be out here after what happened. You need to be safe on the way home."

"Brooke? What's going on? Who's that?"

I turn my attention back to the phone. "It's John. From the bar. I'm okay."

"I'll be there any minute," Cole says.

John nods. "I'll wait here if you want me to. It's better to be safe than sorry."

My eyebrows nearly take off of their own accord. I've only ever known John as the sleazy guy at the bar. I'm still scared, but it's weirdly reassuring that he's prepared to wait with me. "Thank you."

For a second, I'm blinded by the lights of Cole's car, and my heart leaps when he gets out. *He came for me.*

"Ready to go?" There's so much love in his smile.

I nod.

"You take care of our Brooke. She's had a hard time, you know," John says.

*Our Brooke.* I bite down on my lip to stop myself smiling.

"You'd better believe it." Cole smiles. "Thanks for waiting with her."

"If I'd known she was out here, I would have been

here earlier. You be careful." John brushes his hand against my arm, and for the first time ever I don't recoil.

"Thank you, John."

"You're welcome. Glad to see you back." He waves, and wanders off down the street.

Cole stares after him. "That was a bit random."

"He gave me a fright. I thought … I'm just glad you're here."

Cole runs his fingers through my hair. "How about we get you home?"

"I feel so stupid."

"Come here." He wraps his arms around my shoulders. "I'm glad you called. And it's not stupid to be scared. Not after what happened."

I close my eyes.

"Let's go. Rosalyn will be worried."

I nod, wrapping my arms around his waist. "Just hold me for a minute."

"Of course."

In his embrace, I fight back tears at how good this feels. How normal.

He kisses the top of my head. "Let's go."

I pull away from him, but I'm reluctant to do so. Rosalyn will worry if I'm home later than usual, and I need to be near Kaia.

The car's warm, and I lean back in the seat. It feels silly to be driving a block and a half to home.

"Call me any time, day or night, if you need me.

I'll always come." Cole holds my hand in his. This takes me back. So many times he'd drop me off home, and I'd linger in his car as long as possible. But this time, he's the one lingering.

And I don't mind at all.

"Wait there." He gets out of the car and rounds it, opening my door and holding out his hand. "My lady?" He grins.

I roll my eyes, but I'm pretty sure my grin matches his. "What are you doing?"

"Trying to impress you."

"You're doing pretty well already."

"Gotta make sure my lady and my baby are taken care of."

My heart clenches as I take his hand and step out of the car. He pushes the door closed behind me and taps his key to lock it.

He squeezes my hand, and we walk into the building. No more words are said as we ride in the elevator hand in hand, and walk to my apartment door.

"Cole?"

He turns, and my heart's in my throat when I see how sad he looks. My emotions are muddled as it is, but even more so in his presence. "Yes?"

"I just wanted to say thank you."

He gives me a small smile. "Like I said. Call me any time of the day or night. I'll always be here for you and Kaia."

"I really appreciate it. And I appreciate the financial support. I'm not sure if I've said that."

His smile grows. "It's the least you deserve. I want to provide for my family. Especially when I failed last time."

"That wasn't your fault."

There's hope in his expression. "Did you remember that? We haven't had that conversation."

I shake my head. "No. Your father came to see me." Shifting my gaze to my apartment door, I take a deep breath. "Want to come in and talk? Rather than doing it in the hallway?"

He nods. "I'd like to hear about this visit. He promised me he wouldn't harass you."

"That's not what he did." I turn the handle, and Cole follows me through into the living room. Rosalyn's sitting on the couch, her head bowed. She's fast sleep. I can't help but smile.

"Ros." I touch her arm.

"Oh." She jumps. "I was just resting my eyes."

I grin. "I'm sure you were. I'm home now."

She looks up at Cole and smiles. "It's so good to see you, Cole."

"You too, Rosalyn. Has that girl of ours been good?"

Rosalyn nods as she stands. "She's always good. I'm glad you're here." She gives me a pointed look, and I fight the urge to roll my eyes. I appreciate how much she cares, but I don't need any more pressure. I'm giving myself enough of that.

"Good night, Ros."

She smiles. "Good night. See you tomorrow."

And then it's just us, Cole and me, standing in my living room. Something's familiar about this. We've been here before. But I just can't reach the memory.

"I'll make some coffee," I say.

"Is that good for you?"

I narrow my eyes. "Are you really doing that?"

"No. Shit. I meant as a general question. Not as in telling you what to do." He smiles. "It's been a long night. You deserve a coffee."

"I didn't give it up last time."

He nods. "You did. And you replaced your coffee habit with cookie dough ice cream. I swear that's where half the grocery money went."

I laugh.

"It wasn't all bad, was it?" His eyes shine.

"Not all of it." I pause. "I'll go make that coffee."

When I come back with two cups, Cole's sitting on the couch. I like him being here. I can't deny it. While I'm still confused about him, his presence calms me.

"Thanks," he says as I hand him a cup. "What did Dad want?"

I place my mug on the coffee table as I sit. "He wanted to apologize. I learned a lot about his relationship with my father, and then he bought us dinner and hung out with Kaia."

Cole smiles. "He did?"

"Clearly he didn't tell you."

Cole lets out a loud breath. "I haven't spoken to him. We agreed he'd keep his distance until you got your memory back, and we could work out where to go from there."

"Give him a call. I think he misses you." I lick my lips. "He asked me to give you another chance."

"He did?"

I nod. "He has a lot of regrets, and I think the way he handled our relationship from the start is weighing on his mind."

"Did you tell him about the baby?"

"No. He wants us to get back together as it is. I thought that would just add to the pressure."

"You're probably right there."

"Thank you for tonight." I rest my elbow on the back of the couch and run my fingers through my hair. "I don't know what that was all about."

"You were scared. And that's okay."

"I need to move on. I need to get over this and find a way forward."

Cole drains the rest of his coffee and places the cup on the table. "I'll walk you home every night."

I shake my head. "You don't have to do that."

He nods. "I think I do."

My lips twitch as I fight a smile, but I cave, and

Cole's eyes light up as one crosses my lips. "I won't say no, then."

He reaches for my arm. "I'm not trying to push you. I wouldn't have stayed away these weeks if I was. But your safety is really important to me. Especially now. It's hard enough dealing with the impact this thing has had on us, but I won't risk losing you altogether."

I place my hand on his. "You were the only person I thought to call tonight. I knew you'd make me feel safe. Maybe I can't remember what happened between us, but there's something, Cole. I want you to know that."

"It's so hard to walk away from you."

My eyes mist over looking into his.

"I don't know what to do. There's this connection that I feel to you, but I don't know how to process it. The last thing I want to do is to hurt you when you clearly care about me, and that's all I seem to be doing."

He cups my cheek with his other hand. "I'm tough. And I put you through worse for no reason. I'm not going anywhere."

"I don't want to drive you away."

"That's impossible. I want to spend the rest of my life with you, Brooke."

His words take my breath away, and hot tears spill down my cheeks. Cole loves me. It's written in his every word and action.

*Remember.*

"Hey. Don't cry. You need to feel safe with me before you let that barrier down again. I know that. I'll wait as long as I need to."

He doesn't say anything else, but gathers me into his arms. I close my eyes as his head rests against mine.

I do feel safe with him.

But I'm still afraid to take the leap of faith I think I need to.

**8**

---

BROOKE

I'M STILL TIRED. I feel like I'm not in my own skin. There's a gap in my memory, and with everyone treating me differently, it's pressing on my mind.

Jenny still can't do enough to help me. The other day I was a few minutes late and she didn't get upset, and she's been bending over backward to make sure I get my proper breaks. Maybe there's some guilt going on there over how harsh she was before. I'm just glad I still have a job.

Back at the bar, things are just as strange. Eric and Katie are fighting, which doesn't make anything easy. And Craig hovers over me like a concerned parent.

I'm almost thankful things are normal when I feel John's hand on my ass while leaning against the bar. At least some things are back to normal.

"What do you want, John?"

"Just another drink, sweetheart." He leans closer. "If there's anything I can ever do ..."

"I'll keep that in mind." I slide out from his grasp. He was so nice the other night, but at times like this, I'm still repulsed by him.

"I'll get you that drink." Craig speaks from behind the bar. "Brooke, table six just left."

I nod. Table six only had drinks, but there'll be glasses to collect. It's not a busy night, so there's no real hurry, but I appreciate his quick thinking.

An hour later, there are barely any customers, and I stand by the bar sipping water. I can't wait to get home and off my feet.

"Brooke, can I ask you something?" Craig tops up my water.

"Sure."

"So, I was wondering ... He swings on his heels. "I thought maybe we could go out sometime."

I do nothing but blink rapidly, his suggestion blindsiding me. "I appreciate it, Craig, but I don't think so."

"Are you back with Cole?"

I chew the inside of my cheek while I decide whether any of this is his business. "Not yet, but who knows what will happen?"

He nods. "Let me know if you change your mind."

"Sure."

I turn, and see John looking at me from his table.

His eyes are so sad, and while he's his usual gross self, something about him feels different. I'm not sure whether to be scared of him or not.

The police haven't worked out what happened. I'm in the dark about who to be afraid of. Maybe it was a random attack, but the thought of that doesn't make me any less frightened.

I am so grateful to Cole that he's taken to walking me home. Every night I hope that something will prod my memory, but nothing has yet. My heart's warmed by the fact that he walks me home with no expectation. He just cares.

He was right when he said I needed to feel safe with him to let my barrier down. For someone I thought I'd never trust again, he just keeps on proving how dedicated he is to us. Feelings that never really went away begin to bloom, and it gets a little harder every night to say goodbye at my door.

I don't know what feelings are lingering from five years ago, and which are recent. Remnants of memories nag at me, but not enough for me to grab hold of and be sure.

"Hey, babe." I turn to see Cole walk through the door of the bar. "Ready?"

"Let me grab my coat."

His eyes are so full of love. It radiates from him, and I don't need him to tell me how he's feeling to know. I can see it. It's scary and wonderful, and it makes me feel worse for not letting him in to see Kaia.

Even if Cole's not a part of my life, he should be a part of hers. She misses him so much.

Grabbing my coat from my locker, I head back through the bar. Cole helps me put the garment on, and takes my hand in his. No matter our past, he makes me feel safe.

As he usually does, he holds my hand all the way home.

"I've been thinking …" I say.

He nods. "I've done nothing but think."

"You should come and see Kaia." I suck in a deep breath. "Maybe she could stay a night at your place."

His grin lights up his whole face. "I'd love that. I'm not sure if she'd come to my place without you though."

"Well, we could both stay? I'm not working Saturdays anymore, so we could both come."

He reaches for my other hand. "That would be amazing. I can't think of anything I want more."

"Baby steps."

Cole nods. "Whatever it takes."

He plants a lingering kiss on my cheek. I inhale him. Again, it's confusing. He smells the same as he did when we were teenagers. Is the familiarity an old or a new thing?

"See you tomorrow," he murmurs in my ear.

I could cry at how much I want to remember. Instead, I nod. "Tomorrow."

He lets go of my hands, and I pluck my house key out of my bag and slide it into the lock.

"Good night, Brooke."

"Good night."

I close the door, and stand there for a few moments, looking at it. I'm not sure what I'm doing anymore. I don't know if spending a weekend with him is the right thing to do, but it feels like it is.

The thought of telling Kaia puts a grin on my face. She'll be over the moon at the thought of spending time with her daddy. And I'll be happy about it too.

When Ros leaves, I shower and climb into bed, exhausted and ready to sleep. My bed seems cold and empty. *Cole.*

"Mommy." Kaia snuggles under the covers beside me. She wraps her little arms around my neck and hugs me tight. This whole thing must be unsettling for her. She just found out she has family, and I've taken it away from her.

"Kaia, how would you like to spend the weekend with Daddy?"

Her eyes widen. "Can we?"

I nod. "Yes, we can.

I'm not sure if I've ever seen my little girl so excited. She's so happy, and it puts a smile on my face despite the devastation I feel. *This is what I've been withholding from her.*

"Well, we can spend Saturday night with him. And then we'll come home on Sunday."

I kiss her on the temple, and we settle down to sleep.

This kid is my everything. I love her, live for her.

It's time for her to get what she wants too.

## 9

---

BROOKE

Cole picks us up on Saturday. We drive through town, with Kaia pointing out things she recognizes from our daily bus trip.

Cole links his fingers in mine and drags them to his lips. "I don't have any expectations this weekend. I want you to know that. Kaia has her room, and I've sorted out one of the other spare rooms for you to sleep in."

"Thank you." It's weird. I love how considerate he's being, but part of me wishes he'd ask me to sleep in his bed. I know I'd feel secure and loved there.

*One thing at a time.*

"Daddy's house," Kaia sings, and I catch my breath at the sight of Cole's house because of the feeling of déjà vu.

*I've been here.*

It's familiar.

He pulls into the driveway, and smiles at me as I step out of the car and join him on the path leading to the house.

Kaia rushes inside when he opens the door, disappearing up the hallway with her backpack.

"She knows where she's going." I laugh.

"She's in for a surprise. It's a lot different to when you were here last time."

*Last time.* The thought echoes in my heart.

I take a look around. There's not a lot here, but it feels cozy and comfortable. It's so much bigger than my little apartment, though, that's not hard.

"Your home is beautiful."

"*Our* home." He shuffles a little closer. "That's what I hope it'll be, anyway. It just needs you and Kaia."

My heart thuds, our gazes locked. His expression is so open. He's not hiding anything, and the love he feels for both me and our daughter is plain to see. "I'm sorry."

He frowns. "What for?"

"For not remembering." I drop my gaze. "And for not letting you spend time with Kaia. There's nothing wrong with her memory."

He chuckles. "She inherited your smarts."

"I seem to remember you were pretty smart too."

"Were?"

I look back up to see a big grin on his face.

Shrugging, I pull back a bit. "I can't possibly comment on how smart you are now."

"Daddy, look." Kaia emerges from the hallway with the toy Cole's father gave her. It was the first thing in her bag when we packed, she loves it so much.

"You got one? I was going to get one for your birthday," Cole says.

"Grandpa gave it to me."

His eyebrows rise. "Grandpa did?"

"When he came to see us," I say. "He remembered because she saw some ad on television in their motel room."

"I remember her seeing the same ad at your place. Huh. I never thought Dad would pay that close attention to what she was watching though."

"Your father seems very different to the man I knew when we were growing up. He has a lot of regret in his life."

"I never thought I'd hear you defend him."

Kaia turns the dog on and sets it on the floor. It walks for a bit and then falls over.

Cole chuckles. He picks up the remote control and turns on the television.

"I've got a new movie for us to watch, Kaia. Have you seen the Minions movie?"

She shakes her head.

"It's on Netflix. I'll turn it on for you."

Once he's started it up, he turns his attention to me. "Sorry. How did your visit with Dad go?"

"He apologized from the heart. I can't pretend that what he did didn't hurt me, but I can move forward. And Kaia was thrilled to see him."

I suck on my bottom lip. "I'm going to let them see her too. Your mother never did anything wrong, and it's not fair for her to miss out."

Cole's face lights up. "She'll love that. Thank you."

"As confusing as all this is, I need to do what's best for Kaia. I feel bad about keeping you two apart. I didn't mean to hurt either of you. Kaia loves you so much."

Cole reaches out, touching my cheek with his fingertips. "You're only doing what you think is right. I can't say I was happy about it, but it is what it is. You can't force yourself to remember."

"I wish I could. I'm not sure what hurts the most: my pain at not remembering, or yours from me keeping you at arm's length."

He cups my face. "Not quite arm's length anymore."

I can't help but grin as he presses his forehead to mine.

"Mommy. Daddy. Shhh." Kaia holds her index finger to her lips, and we laugh.

As the movie starts, Cole slips his arm around my shoulders. I lean in to him. It's instinctive. It's natural. It feels right.

*The scent of popcorn.*

*Cuddles on the couch with Cole while Kaia watches movies.*

It's so close, but I can't reach it. It's not a memory, but a feeling.

"Brooke? You okay?" Cole's voice is full of concern.

"Have we done this before?"

He nods. "It's one of the things we did when I was trying to win you over. I bought Kaia a heap of DVDs, and we had a movie day."

"That's where all those DVDs came from."

"Kaia didn't tell you?"

I shrug. "I just assumed we'd got them on special. What else did we do?"

"We were in the routine of me dropping you off at work and day care, and then picking you up when you were finished. Then, I'd stay with Kaia while you worked nights. And then …" There's a glint in his eye as he leans closer. "Well, you can use your imagination for that."

I slap his arm. "Stop teasing me."

"Nearly every night we were together. And extra on Sundays when we had the whole evening together and Kaia was asleep."

My cheeks burn. "Nearly every night, huh?"

"We couldn't keep our hands off each other."

I have no doubt he's telling the truth.

And not remembering hurts even more.

Kaia's up way past her bedtime, but her joy at family time makes it worth it.

I let Cole be the father. He helps Kaia change into her pajamas and tucks her into bed. He reads her a bedtime story. He goes to get that glass of water she uses as a tactic to spend a little more time with him.

I love watching them together.

When Cole emerges from her room, his smile is a mile wide.

"Thank you," he whispers.

"For what?"

"Letting me do that. I loved putting her to bed when you were working. I've missed it."

I take a deep breath. "Well, I have this weird feeling at night. Like there's something missing. I think it's you."

He runs his thumb over the back of my hand. "I hope it is."

"I just don't know what to do, Cole."

For a moment, he's silent, and he licks his lips slowly, as if he's trying to work out what to say. "You don't have to do anything. We'll just keep on going the way we have been, and one day we'll find our way back." Pain flickers across his expression. "Or we won't. But either way, we'll make sure Kaia has us both, and that she knows she's loved."

I nod. "Maybe we can set up some type of arrangement."

"I said I wouldn't try for custody, and I stand by that. You have your routine with Kaia, and I don't want to interfere." He squeezes my hand. "Unless I get part-time custody of you too."

"What do you mean?" I laugh.

"I mean, the three of us spend time together. Just like this. If you're working five nights a week, maybe you can spend the weekends with me. There are four rooms here. We don't have to share a bed, just like we're not tonight." He sighs. "We'll make it work."

I pull my hand from his and throw my arms around his neck.

"Woah." He plants a kiss on my neck, and I gasp. *So good.* "Shit. Sorry. Just instinctive."

"It's okay. I just wanted to say thank you."

"You've already said that enough."

"But I mean it. I know you could be difficult with all of this, but you're being patient and caring, and I really appreciate it."

He wraps his arms around me, pulling me closer. "I'll admit it's not easy, but I figure you're worth the wait."

"I hope so."

"Go and say good night to our daughter." He kisses my temple, and it's with great reluctance that we pull apart. I like the way he makes me feel.

Kaia's room is magic. The projected stars slowly

move across the ceiling, and I watch them for a moment before sitting on the side of the bed. I pull the blanket up and make sure she's tucked in before leaning over to kiss her temple.

I leave her room, walking up the hall and to the left, where Cole's spare room is. As I pass his bedroom door, I look up. He's standing beside the bed, tugging his shirt over his head.

Seeing him gives me the same feelings I had at eighteen. I loved watching him play sport, or do chores with no shirt on, but now he's older, more defined. His solid chest leads down to his abs that leave me wondering what it's like to touch them. To run my finger over the peaks and valleys down to that deep *V* above his sweatpants.

As I run my gaze back up, he meets it, and there's so much heat in his expression that I retreat, dropping my head to look at the floor.

"Good night, Brooke."

He's so close and yet so far.

I scuttle into the bedroom and say a quick "good night" before closing the door behind me.

Why can't this be simple? Why can't I just go to him and ask for his help remembering? He loves me, and he wants to make love to me. It's in his every gesture, his every touch—even the incidental ones.

I can't deny that I want him too.

But I'm scared.

I fight myself constantly when it comes to Cole.
I curl up on the bed and cry myself to sleep.

**10**

---

BROOKE

LATE SUNDAY AFTERNOON he drops us home. We've had a good weekend. Kaia's had both of us, and milked it for all it was worth. But it's been so good to see her smiling.

She disappears to her room when we walk in the door, and I flop on the couch.

Cole walks toward me. "Can I hang around for a bit?"

I nod. "Can't see why not. Thank you for this weekend."

"It was great. I hope you both had fun."

I nod. "What are you doing tomorrow?"

"Working. Why?"

I bite down on my bottom lip. "I wondered if you would come to my neurologist appointment with me."

"What time?" He sits beside me on the couch.

"My appointment's at one."

He smiles. "Of course I will. Thank you for letting me in on it."

"I have another appointment straight after, and I thought you might like to come to that too."

His smile widens. "What kind of appointment?"

"Well, I let the neurologist know about my pregnancy, and he got me an appointment with an OB/GYN at the hospital. Just to make sure everything's okay."

I gasp as he presses his lips to mine. It's not unwelcome, but it is unexpected, and he recoils, his eyes wide.

"Shit. Sorry. I just got carried away with the thought of our baby."

"It's okay. They might do an ultrasound. I mean, it'll be tiny, but I want you to be there if we do."

He nods. "I wouldn't miss it for the world." His eyes grow sad, and I don't have to ask to know he's thinking about all the time he missed with Kaia. He was with me during the pregnancy, and for Kaia's ultrasounds, but after that … "Can we get a picture, do you think?"

I shrug. "We can ask."

"There's no way I want to miss a thing. Now or in the future."

"Of course."

He places his hand on my stomach. "I still can't believe we're having another baby. The little one must be strong to have survived what he or she has. I know you're okay now apart from the memory loss, but I keep thinking about how that car hit you."

"We'll have to see how things go." I look at him from under my eyelashes. "I'm glad you're here with me."

"Me too. I've missed so much of your life. It's hard to think about missing out on any more. I'll be here the whole way, Brooke." He frowns. "Dad's paying your medical bills. Won't he get billed for the OB/GYN? Then he'll know," Cole says.

I shrug. "I'm not sure."

"Or I'll just sort out that part of the bill myself."

I shake my head. "You don't have to. I'm sure I have enough in the bank."

"This is my baby too. I'll pay the bill."

"Okay, okay." I smile.

"Have you told Kaia about the baby yet?"

"Not yet. I want to hold off for a while. Let us get our heads around it first."

He nods.

"And then we'll tell her together."

He grins as Kaia reappears, her arms full of toys.

"I should probably go. Let you guys get settled in for the night," Cole says.

I nod.

"See you tomorrow. Want me to pick you up from work?"

"That would be good."

"I'll be there about twelve thirty. That'll give us plenty of time to get to the neurologist and work out what we're doing." He leans over and pecks me on the cheek before standing.

"Now, give me a hug before I go." He squats, holding his arms open for Kaia.

She throws herself into them with all the dramatic finesse of a four-year-old.

"I love you." He presses a kiss into her hair.

"Love you, Daddy."

"Be a good girl for Mommy, and I'll see you again soon." He extracts her fingers from his hair where she's entangled them, and stands.

Saying goodbye is so hard. So much harder than I ever imagined it would be. I open my mouth to speak, but I can't find the words and close it again.

With a nod, he opens the door and walks out, closing it without saying another word. I let out a long breath.

Something about this is so wrong, but I don't know what to do.

"Is Daddy coming back?" Kaia asks.

"Not today, sweetheart. Another day."

Her lower lip wobbles. "Are we going to his house?"

"We're home now. He's going to his home. We'll see him again really soon."

Tears roll down her cheeks, and she hammers on the door. "Daddy."

"How about we put on some cartoons and I'll make a hot chocolate?"

"Popcorn and movies with Daddy." She folds her arms, and stamps one of her feet on the ground.

"Not today. Come on." I hold out my hand, but she turns her head. "Kaia. Behave. You'll see him again really soon. I'll talk to him and maybe we can go and see him in his house again."

When she just stands there, I walk away, flopping on the couch and flicking on the television.

"Daddy," she wails.

My heart shatters. Is this what I've done to her? Caused her this much pain? I knew how much Kaia loved Cole, but my little girl just sounds heartbroken.

"Kaia, it's okay. We'll see Daddy again really soon."

She lets out another cry, and it pierces me to the gut.

"You know what? Let's forget that. I think you're tired and need a sleep. I know I am." I stand and walk over to her, pick her up, and carry her to her room. She doesn't protest, but that lower lip of hers juts out as I strip off her clothes and pull on her pajamas.

"Kaia, Mommy's really tired right now, and I need you to be good. You can sleep in my bed if you want."

She puts all her weight down, and I pick her up

rather than dragging her into my room. I pull her onto the bed, and we snuggle under the covers.

"Daddy." She lets out a loud wail, and I sigh.

"Come on, Kaia."

She sobs, and I can't stand it anymore. I get back out of bed and head to the couch where my bag is.

I pull out my phone, dialing Cole. I'm tired, and I need his support now more than ever.

"Hey," he answers, and I hear the echo of the phone being on Bluetooth. He's not even home yet.

"Cole, can you please come back?"

"Sure. What's up?"

"Kaia's distraught. I've never seen her like this. She wants you."

"On my way."

The phone disconnects, and I'm left staring at it.

Back in the bedroom, Kaia's sobbing. It breaks my heart to see her like this.

I climb into bed, still fully clothed, and wrap myself around her.

It doesn't help.

Nothing helps.

I lie in silence while she cries beside me. She won't let me comfort her. This is it. She's reached her breaking point.

I look up as the door rattles, and Cole walks into the bedroom. He has a key? This whole time he's had a key to my place?

He meets my gaze. "Sorry if I hung up on you. I didn't mean to."

He looks at Kaia. "What are you doing?"

"Daddy." She sniffles as he lies down beside her.

He reaches over her and squeezes my hand before gathering her into his arms. "What's all this about?"

"I miss you."

He smiles, stroking her cheek with the tip of his index finger. "We just spent the weekend together."

"Daddy." She doesn't say anything else, but she snuggles in against his chest. There's nothing else to say, I guess. She's got her father here, and all is right in her world.

I wish I could say the same for mine.

Guilt hangs over me as I watch them. I did this to them. I kept them apart when they wanted to be together. I'm the odd one out right now, and it hurts so much.

"You have to be good for Mommy," Cole says. "She's still getting better after being in the hospital, and she needs you to take care of her. This isn't taking care of her, is it, Kaia?" He lets go of her, and she rolls over to look at me.

I force a smile, and plant a kiss on her forehead.

"I just miss Daddy."

"I know you do, sweetheart. And I'm sorry. I know how much you love him."

She nods. "I love you too."

I cup her cheek. "We both love you very, very much."

She rolls back and snuggles in tighter with her father. I stare at the ceiling as Kaia's breathing evens out.

"Brooke," Cole whispers. "Want me to leave?"

"You don't have to. Thank you for coming back."

He reaches over Kaia, and runs his hand down my arm. "I know things are hard right now. I'll try and make them easier when I can."

"I appreciate it."

"If you want to move into my place, you're always welcome. You need to get your rest, and I'll always be there to be with Kaia."

"I'll think about it."

We spend the night sleeping in the same bed with Kaia between us.

And I sleep better than I have in weeks.

WHEN I OPEN MY EYES, it's morning. And a lot lighter in my room than it should be.

I turn to look at the clock.

*Shit.*

It's 10:05 a.m.

Cole and Kaia are nowhere to be seen.

"Cole?"

I scramble from my bed, darting down the hall.

He's sitting at the dining table with a smile on his face.

"I'm so late for work. Why did you let me sleep so long? Where's Kaia?"

"Relax. Kaia's at day care. You were clearly exhausted. I called Jenny and told her you weren't coming in. Then I called Marcus and told him the same thing."

My hands fly to my hips. "Why would you do that? You can't make that kind of decision for me."

"You look so much like your mother." He laughs, and I know he's not meaning anything malicious, but it doesn't help my mood. "We get to see our baby today, and I thought it might be better if you were more relaxed. I don't know. I was only trying to help."

"By causing me stress over missing work?"

"Come here and have some breakfast. How's the morning sickness?"

I sit at the table and cross my arms. "Fine."

"Toast? Or do you think you can stomach some bacon? There's plenty there. I stopped at the store on the way home."

"Were you this pushy before?"

He nods. "I've always been pushy. You know that."

His easy manner and the smile he has on his face relaxes me. My anger diminishes. I can't stay angry with him when he's showing me how much he cares.

I laugh. "Well, that much is true. And toast would be good. I'm feeling okay, but I don't want to risk upsetting my stomach."

"Fair enough. I'll make you a coffee too."

"Thanks, Cole."

He walks around the table, and places one hand at the back of my neck. I close my eyes. "You're welcome. If you're really lucky, I'll rub your back when we get home from the hospital. You're so tense."

Tears prick my eyes as he walks to the kitchen. It still pisses me off that he made the decision to leave me to sleep, but he's trying to be sweet and protective.

Besides, the extra sleep was nice.

"Was Kaia okay this morning?" I ask.

He nods. "She was fine. I think she had a big weekend, and she was tired last night."

"She's feeling the strain of all of this. It's not fair on her."

Cole walks toward me, placing a cup of coffee on the table. "No, it's not. But we just have to work through this like we have been. It'll take time."

I nod. "I guess you're right. You're so good with her."

"I hate that I wasn't a part of her life for so long. There's so much I want to make up to you both."

"You're doing well at that. I really do appreciate you coming back yesterday."

"I'd do anything for her."

"I know you would."

He sits beside me at the table. "We've got some time until your first appointment. Have your coffee and go back to bed if you want. I can just watch TV or something until you wake up."

I smile. "You know what? I think I might."

Cole places his hand on mine. "I'd do anything for you too."

"I know."

THE NEUROLOGIST DOESN'T KEEP us waiting long. He smiles as we're shown into his office. "Brooke, it's good to see you. You're looking well."

"I'm not feeling too bad, though the morning sickness is a bit up and down."

His smile widens. "That's right. You've got an appointment with an OB today too, haven't you?"

I nod. "After this."

"Well, I won't keep you too long. If you could sit on the exam table, I'll just check a couple of things and run a few tests."

He tests my reflexes, and shines lights in my eyes. His smile tells me he hasn't found anything to worry about.

"Hop down. Everything's looking good. How's the memory?"

I take a seat next to Cole by the doctor's desk. "I still have this gap. Sometimes it's like things try to break through, but it's more feelings than anything solid."

"What's the last thing you remember before waking up in hospital?" he asks.

I shrug. "It's difficult to say. I've kept to the same routine for so long, the days kind of blur into one another. I remember going to work, dropping Kaia at day care, picking her up, having dinner, going to my night job ..."

He nods. "It might take a while for the detail to come back. And then again, it might not come back at all."

I shoot a glance at Cole. "I just feel like I've missed out on so much. Cole and I got back together, and I can't remember any of it."

"That's the difficult part. The things we want to remember are buried with the things we don't. Something traumatic happened the night you were hit by the car, and your mind could be shielding you from that."

I lick my lips. "And there's nothing I can do about it?"

"Time is the best medicine. The scans looked good when you were discharged. Everything's healing the way it should. It's a matter of the brain making those connections it dropped when you had the bleed."

"I thought so. I just hoped there was some shortcut."

"I'm sorry, but there's not."

I let out a sigh. "It was worth asking."

"So, from here, we'll do another CT scan and a checkup in three months. Please contact me if you do have your memory return in the meantime."

I nod. "Of course."

"Good luck, Brooke."

When we leave the office, Cole grabs my hand. "That was good."

"Was it? What if I never remember?"

He shrugs. "I don't know."

"I want to remember. Not just because of us, but because I want to know who chased me that night. What if it's someone I know? Or what if whoever it was comes back to make sure I don't tell anyone who did it? I want the police to be able to do something."

Tears roll down my cheeks.

"Hey." Cole opens his arms and I fall into them, the tears escalating into full-blown sobs.

I stand in the hospital corridor, crying, with my husband's arms around me.

"How about we go and see our baby?" he says softly.

I pull back. His eyes are so full of love.

"I could do with something good."

"It is good. Isn't it?" His eyes search mine.

Nodding, I take a deep breath. "Scary, but I'm not as freaked out as I was."

He takes my hand in his. "I'm right here the whole way."

"I know."

---

"How far along do you think you are?" Doctor McGregor asks.

"Nine or ten weeks? It must have happened just before the accident because I haven't had sex since then."

"If we perform an ultrasound, it'll help us firm up the dates for you. I know you must be anxious after everything you've been through. It's still early days, but it's a good sign that you've got this far."

I nod. "Seeing the baby might make this feel real too. It's all crazy right now."

"I'm sure." He gives me a reassuring smile, and Cole reaches over to take my hand. I'm so glad he's with me. But it's weird when you can't remember the activities leading to conceiving a baby.

"Come this way." He walks around his desk and opens a door to an adjoining room.

I take a deep breath, and Cole squeezes my hand as we step through. When we were having Kaia, we had a scan much later on.

I climb onto the bed, and the doctor lifts my shirt.

"I'll just put some gel on and we'll get started." He smiles.

I nod. "I remember from when I had Kaia."

The gel hits, and I suck in a breath. This is it. We're going to see the baby.

"Everything okay?" Doctor McGregor asks.

I nod. "Fine."

"This shouldn't take too long." He runs the wand across my stomach. It's hard to believe there's anything in there. I move my gaze to the monitor above the bed.

It takes a moment.

"Here we go."

The ultrasound is grainy, but there's definitely something there. There's a flash on the screen. A heartbeat. A sign of life.

*Our baby.*

"Right now, your baby is an inch and quarter long. Your ten week guess is pretty close."

I blink rapidly. This is overwhelming. I never had a scan this early with Kaia, but then again, I remembered everything when it came to her creation.

*I'm going to be a mother again.*

I shift my gaze to Cole.

*We're going to be parents again.*

There's still this gap in my mind that's driving me

crazy. I want to remember. I want to feel the love this baby was created with. It's unfair. It's so unfair.

Cole grips my hand tight, and I smile at the grin on his face. He's happy. He's proud. We might be apart, but I feel closer to him than ever. This is my husband and the father of my children, and I can't deny that I love him. Not anymore.

The thought alone makes me giddy.

We're patching our family back together, piece by piece.

## 11

BROOKE

WE DRIVE BACK to my place in silence. Seeing the child growing inside me has been overwhelming, and I lean against the car window, looking out of it but not really seeing.

"Want to pick Kaia up on the way? We can if you want."

I look at the car clock. It's 3:30 p.m. "We could do."

"Or I can drive you home, and come back and get her. Give us some time alone at home."

I nod. "That'd be good for just a little while.

"The ultrasound was amazing. The technology, I mean. Being able to see something that small. And that heartbeat. I wish we'd seen Kaia at that stage."

"Kaia's going to be over the moon when we do tell her about the baby."

He laughs. "She'll make such a good big sister."

"If she doesn't smother the baby with love." I smile. "She's going to be so happy and excited. Maybe it'll distract her from everything else that's going on."

"Or it could confuse her further. Let's wait a little longer to tell her."

As we pull up outside my place, I look at Cole. "You're right. There's enough going on without adding something else to the mix. It's confusing enough for me."

We walk into my apartment, and I throw myself at the couch.

Cole chuckles. "Why don't you take a nap?"

"I think I slept enough for the day." I sit, and he joins me.

He leans closer. "I'm here. I can pick up Kaia and cook dinner if you want me to."

"Cole, you don't have—"

"I know I don't have to. I want to." He licks his lips. "There's something else I need to run by you."

"What?"

"I thought we might go out for dinner one night. It worked well last time." He smiles.

"Worked well for what?"

"It gave us time to spend together. I mean, we can sit here and wait for Kaia to go to bed, but it'd be nice to get out. Just the two of us."

"I like that idea."

"Maybe Rosalyn could look after Kaia for a couple of hours. While we sneak off."

*Kaia.*

I nod. "I like that idea. I'm not sure how Kaia's going to react the next time you leave."

He licks his lips. "I don't have to leave. I could always sleep on your couch for a few nights."

"She'll still be upset the night you don't."

Cole sighs. "What do we do?"

"I don't know." I bite down tears. "I feel like I'm letting everyone down right now. You, Kaia, my work …"

He palms my cheek, and I close my eyes. "You're really not. Kaia's too young to understand what's going on. She just got her father back and now she probably feels like she's lost him again. But that's not your fault."

"I know, but it still hurts."

Cole pulls me into his arms. "No one could have predicted what happened. My concern is to keep you safe. And I'll do whatever I can to do that."

"Thank you."

"Why don't you rest, and I'll go and get Kaia? I might even bring home some takeout instead of cooking." He stands, and I lie back on the couch. "Maybe you're not my girl right now, but I think it's still my job to take care of you. That's my baby you're carrying."

I nod. "I appreciate it."

His expression is pained for a moment. This whole thing must be a huge strain on him. He thought he had his family back only for it all to fall apart. The longer I dwell on it, the more selfish I feel.

I close my eyes, and drift off to sleep as he leaves.

I'm not sure how long I'm out, but I wake to the sound of the door opening.

Kaia's all smiles as she walks in, hand in hand with Cole.

"Daddy's going to sleep at his house tonight," she announces as she snuggles next to me.

"Is he now?" I glance at Cole, who has his own wide smile.

She nods. "But he said he'll read me a story before bed first."

I lean over and press a kiss to her forehead. "That's good. And you're happy with that?"

She looks up at Cole and purses her lips. He cocks an eyebrow in return. They've done some kind of deal. It's written all over her face.

"Kaia's a big girl now, and she knows if she's good then good things happen. Right, Kaia?" Cole asks.

Kaia nods.

"I'm going to unpack dinner. I got Chinese. I know you like that sweet and sour pork. Kaia, want to help me?"

"You didn't have to get dinner."

He leans over and kisses my forehead. "Stay there and rest. It's been a big day."

"So bossy," I grumble.

"So bossy." He chuckles as he follows Kaia into the kitchen.

As bossy as he is, it's nice to lie back down on the couch. And it's nice to be fussed over.

I like it.

———

"I should go."

Cole not only sorted out dinner, but he gave Kaia her bath and got her into bed while I laid on the couch. As annoyed as I was over him organizing for me to have the day and night off, I have to admit it's nice not to worry about going to work.

"Thank you for everything today. But I do have one question." I slip off the couch and stand in front of him as he walks back in after kissing Kaia good night.

"What's that?"

"What did you promise her?"

"I told her we could have a movie day at my place. The three of us."

I grip his arm. "Thank you. I don't know if I could deal with the crying every night. Not at the moment."

"Hopefully we'll just ride this out, and things will

all come together." He pecks me on the cheek. "I'll get going and let you get to bed. I'm sure you're tired."

"Thank you for everything."

His eyes light up. "We saw our baby today, Brooke. I can't tell you how excited and happy I am. Thank you for letting me come with you."

"No matter what happens, we're in this together."

He nods. "Yes. We are. Good night."

"Good night."

I close the door behind him when he leaves and lean against it. I've been strong when it comes to our daughter until now, but then, Kaia is usually such a good little girl. Now she's hurt and confused, though apparently open to bribery.

That makes me smile.

I just hope he doesn't break her heart.

# 12

## COLE

It's Thursday, and tonight I'm taking my wife out for dinner. Brooke secured a night off while Marcus is still being lenient with her leave. She's giving me another chance, and I'm not about to waste it.

I take a deep breath and knock on the door.

Brooke answers. She's dressed in a white dress with red flowers all over it. I told her to dress up a little as we're not going to that bar again.

"You look beautiful."

She smiles. "Thank you."

"Don't worry about staying out late," Rosalyn calls.

I laugh. "I'm sure we won't."

"Bye, Mommy." Kaia runs to the door and hugs Brooke's leg. "Daddy."

I pick her up, balancing her on my hip. "How's my girl?"

"Can I come with you?"

I shake my head. "Not this time. We're going to a grown-up restaurant. But next time, I'll take you to McDonald's. Just don't tell your mother."

"She's right here, silly." She laughs.

I kiss her on the nose. "Be good for Rosalyn, and I'll see you really soon. I promise."

For a moment, I look to the heavens and pray she'll be good. I'm not sure how much Brooke can take if Kaia acts out.

"Okay, Daddy." She sighs, but doesn't complain when I drop her back down.

"Love you."

She blows me a kiss, and I can't help but grin.

I take Brooke's hand, and she gives Kaia and Rosalyn one final wave before we leave.

"Where are we going?" she asks.

"There's a small Italian restaurant I wanted to try out. And I know you love spaghetti and meatballs."

The corners of her mouth twitch. "You remembered."

"I remember a lot more about you than you probably realize."

"I wish I remembered what happened before the accident." We're not even at the elevator yet, and her eyes are swimming with tears.

"I know. You will."

MIKE TOLD me about this place. It's romantic with soft lighting, and quiet. I'm not sure how he knows about it. It doesn't sound like his kind of restaurant. But I appreciated the recommendation.

"Apparently the food is amazing," I say.

"I'm looking forward to it." Brooke grins.

The more time we spend together, the more she wants to remember. I guess that's a good sign either way. If the memory of us comes back, she might also get answers as to who was after her that night. Then, maybe we can put all this behind us.

The waitress shows us to a table and gives us a menu each. I order two plates of spaghetti, a beer, and a lemonade as requested by Brooke.

I reach for Brooke's hand.

"You can ask me anything, you know. That's what tonight is about," I say.

She sucks in her bottom lip, then releases it. "How did we end up back together?"

"I hired an investigator to track you down. Dad didn't tell me where you were. And you didn't trust me at first. Especially where Kaia was concerned."

She nods. "I understand that."

"But you gave me an inch. And I proved myself, and showed you just how much I love you."

Her expression softens. "Cole."

"It's true. I know you don't want to hear it, but I love you. And you love me. You just need to remember."

Her eyes turn sad. "I'm sorry I don't remember."

"You will in time. I know it. Things were really different between us. We connected on a whole other level to what we did when we were younger."

"It wasn't all that long ago."

I shake my head. "No. It feels like a lifetime since then, though."

The waitress brings the drinks to the table, and nods at me. "Your meal isn't far away."

"Thank you," I say.

When it arrives, the helpings are so generous that we could have had a plate between us. Brooke's eyes light up.

"Hungry?"

"Starving. The baby wants it."

I laugh. "You used to say that with Kaia."

"I didn't even know you noticed." She frowns. "Sorry. I didn't mean that the way it came out."

"You didn't feel appreciated by me. I know that."

She nods.

"This was something else we realized. Back then our communication was awful. Turns out we've both improved in that respect."

Her lips twitch. "Me more than you."

"You are in so much trouble when we get home." I laugh.

She licks her lips as if hesitating to say the next sentence. "I hope so."

My mouth falls open. "You did not say that."

"I think I did." The light is low, but she's blushing.

I don't want to make her feel uncomfortable, so I look at the giant plates of food. "We should eat before our food gets cold."

"Yes, boss."

I laugh. "You're being very flirtatious."

"I like being out with you. We didn't get to do this before."

"Before?"

"Before Kaia."

I nod. "I like being out with you too."

---

WE TALK ALL EVENING, reminiscing about the past, never touching on the future. Who knows what that will bring?

I drive her home, and it's with great reluctance that we stop outside her apartment.

I hate that we're at her door.

I hate that I'm saying good night.

I hate everything about this.

But I'll do whatever I have to do.

Brooke sucks in her top lip. I want to kiss her so badly it hurts. She's right there and untouchable.

"Well, good night," I say.

She pauses. "Are you going to kiss me good night?"

"Sure." I lean in and peck her on the cheek.

"I was thinking a bit more than that." Her hot breath is near my ear, and my cock stirs.

"You want me to *kiss you* kiss you?"

She nods. "Maybe it'll help trigger a memory. I don't know. I'm desperate."

I lick my lips, cupping her face in my hands.

"It's not just about my memory. I want you to kiss me," she whispers.

There's need in her eyes. I'm not sure if it's for me or part of her search for the past.

I start the kiss gently, sweeping my tongue across the seam of her lips. They part, and I probe her mouth. I'm slow at first. She moans. Unsure of how much she wants, I pull away.

"Keep going." She's breathless. I don't know if this is helping her memory, but it feels so good. It feels like I'm home again.

This time, I plunder her mouth. Placing my palm in the middle of her spine, I pull her hard into me. If she wants to be kissed, I can at least make it one to remember.

I've missed her so much.

When the kiss comes to an end, she looks at me with wide eyes. Without asking, I drop my focus to her jaw, peppering it with kisses before gently sucking on her neck.

She gasps. "Cole. Stop."

I pull away. "Do you really want me to stop?"

She shakes her head. "No. But you should. This is a little too much."

"Did kissing me help?"

Brooke shrugs. "It was nice. Really nice." Tears form in her eyes. "It just made me want to remember even more."

"You were hesitant about us to start with last time. I don't blame you for that. And I'm sorry if I got a little carried away, but I miss you so much."

She nods. "I know. I liked it. I told you to stop because this is still all confusing. It's like living in a fog sometimes." Brooke places her hands in mine. "I do want us to be together, and I want us to be a family. But I need to take it slow."

My heart swells. We're so close, and as frustrating as it is, I'll do whatever she wants. "I understand. You get inside and give Kaia a hug and kiss for me. I'll pick you up from work tomorrow night."

She smiles. "I'd like that."

After a peck on the cheek, I go.

I hate this.

WHEN I GET HOME, I take out the large plastic sheets I bought and cover the floor, moving the bed to the feature wall side of the room.

Setting up the roller, I crack open the can of pale pink paint. Kaia's going to love it. She can have her feature wall on one side, and I'll paint the other three walls.

I paint until the sun peeps through the curtains, then stand in the center of the room, looking around. I've still got more to do, and once it's dry it'll need another coat.

I drop the roller into the tray and sigh. It's time to have a shower and a coffee, and get to work. Today will be long, but the thought of my little girl's smile makes it all worth it. This has to be perfect.

By midday, I'm yawning.

"Another late night?" Mike asks.

I nod. "I'm having trouble sleeping. I took Brooke out to dinner last night and we talked, but I still have to say good night at the end of the evening and go home alone."

"Painting out your sexual frustration?"

"How did you know I was painting?"

"There's a blob of pink paint on the back of your hand."

I look and laugh. "Guess I missed that. I'm still decorating Kaia's room."

"That little girl is gonna live in a palace by the time you've finished."

"She deserves one. The past few years have been hard on her and her mother."

"I hope you're still up for tonight."

"What's tonight?"

His eyebrows shoot up. "Company function."

I let out an exasperated sigh. With everything that's been going on, I completely forgot about our work drinks. Some of my biggest clients will be there, and I can't afford to miss it. Not when my mind hasn't exactly been on work lately. "Shit."

"Got your suit?"

I nod. "I'll just have to go home and get changed."

Mike sits on the couch. "How are things going with Brooke?"

"Better. How are things going with Liz?"

"She's coming as my date tonight."

I grin. "I'm impressed."

Mike sighs. "Seeing you with all you're dealing with … maybe it's time I tried something serious again."

"That's a big step for you."

"I'm just following your lead." He grins.

"Brooke wants us to be family, but she doesn't want to rush."

Mike leans forward. "That's a good start."

"Kaia started playing up when I'm not around. She got so wound up crying for me after I dropped them home the other night."

He frowns. "Is she okay?"

I shake my head. "It's forced us both to look at what we're doing to her. I mean, we're dealing with all this grown-up stuff that Kaia can't comprehend. All she knows is that she had her father back in her life, and then she didn't see him for weeks. No wonder she's clingy."

"Hopefully things will settle down a bit now if you and Brooke are seeing each other more often."

"I hope so."

---

WORK FINISHES AT FIVE, but I've got paperwork to catch up on and don't get out until six thirty. The function isn't until eight thirty, so I've got time to swing past the bar first. Brooke will already be at work, and I want her to know I'm not just skipping out on her for the night.

She smiles as I walk in the door.

"You're here early." She pecks me on the cheek.

"I'm here to tell you that I forgot I have a work thing tonight. I wish I'd remembered earlier because you could have come with me."

"Next time."

I look over at Craig. "Can you please walk Brooke home tonight? I've got this business function I have to go to, and I don't know if I'll be finished in time. They tend to go really late."

He nods. "Sure."

Brooke rolls her eyes. "I'll be fine, guys. I appreciate your concern, but …"

"I'm not putting you at risk again. And I'm not apologizing for being overprotective."

She stabs at my chest with her index finger. "That's fine, because I kind of like it."

I press a kiss to her lips. "I'll see you tomorrow. Give Kaia a hug for me."

"I will. She's with Rosalyn for the night having a sleepover with Ros's grandchildren."

"So you have the night to yourself? Nice." I grin. "I could swing by later?"

"I'll be asleep as soon as my head hits the pillow. It's been a long week."

I chuckle. "Fair enough. Love you."

She gives me a small wave. I hate leaving. Things have shifted between us, and I want so desperately to build on that.

I drive home to change, smiling as I pass Kaia's room. Maybe I can convince Brooke to come and spend the weekend with me. I want her to start seeing the house as our home, and I can't wait to show Kaia the changes to her room.

Checking the time, I go straight to the bedroom. It's been a while since I dressed up this much. I usually wear a suit to work, but this is black-tie formal.

As I'm pulling everything I need out of the wardrobe, a small box falls from a shelf. I suck in a breath. It's the box I put my wedding ring in. When I thought Brooke was gone and wanted nothing to do with me, I took my ring off and hid it away. Now, I push open the box and lift out the gold ring.

At nineteen, wearing it felt weird and awkward. Now it feels right. Like I should never have taken it off.

I smile, grab my shirt and jacket, and close the door.

Next event like this, I'll have my wife on my arm. I can just see the joy she'd have dressing up for the night and then, of course, I'd get to peel her dress off afterward.

It leaves me thinking of the night we conceived Kaia, and the dress Brooke's mother paid for. It seemed to take forever to get her out of it, I was that careful not to tear it. She looked ethereal that night, and it was as if there was a spell cast over me.

I screw my face up at the thought of wrecking everything.

That's in the past, and we're moving forward again.

Things can only get better from here.

---

THE ROOM IS CROWDED. It's the richest of the rich in here, and there's plenty of alcohol on tap. By the end of the night, this is going to be messy.

I'm going to stick to water. I'd rather have a clear head.

"Cole." Barrett, my biggest client, walks toward me. He's got a huge smile on his face, and a tall blonde on his arm. "Darling, this is the man who's helped me go from being rich to being very rich this year. Cole, this is my wife, Alana."

"Nice to meet you."

She casts her gaze down to my hand where my wedding ring shines. "Is your wife here?"

I shake my head. "No, she couldn't make it."

"Pity."

As they walk past me, she runs her index finger over my shoulder blade. I roll my eyes. I've heard there's a bit of that sort of thing that goes on at these parties. But there's no way I'm taking part.

I can't wait until tonight is over.

---

## 13

BROOKE

I love Cole. I can't help it.

Memory or not, I'm falling for him again. He hasn't missed a step, and he's trying so hard to show me how much he wants me. Wants us.

It's close to midnight, and the last patron just left. I'm helping Craig clean up and then I'm going home to sleep.

"Damn it."

Two words.

That's all it takes.

I freeze. Something breaks through the fog. *Pinned to the table, fighting off hands on my waistband. The button on my shorts.*

Turning, I stare at Craig wide-eyed. If he's noticed, he's not said anything, but he's picking up broken glass from the floor.

"Lucky no one trod on this." He looks up. "What's wrong?"

I take a step back.

"Brooke?" His expression falls. "Shit."

"I'm just tired. I'll be glad to go home." I force a smile.

"You know."

"I know what?" My voice shakes, and I know he knows that I know.

He drops the piece of glass back onto the floor and lunges for me. There's no time to get away. He grabs my arms and forces me up against the wall. His hot breath is on my neck, and I grimace as I feel his erection through his pants. He's getting off on this.

"I thought you were dead at first. Then I found out you lost your memory, and I knew I had another chance. But once again, that ex of yours hangs around like a bad smell."

*Cole.*

"We've been growing close, Brooke. I just need a little more time for us."

I can't push him off. He's too strong. "There is no us."

"But there could have been. And then when I tried to take what was mine, you freed yourself of him only to get tied up with him again."

Tears pour down my cheeks. "Cole's my husband."

"You fucked that other guy. That boyfriend you had when I first met you. Cole meant nothing to you then." His weight is pressed against me, and he slips his hand down between us.

"Let's see if this button's a bit more co-operative this time."

My heart's in my throat. I can't move. He's trapped me against the wall, and I can't stop shaking in fear. I suck in air, but it feels like it's going nowhere. My breathing accelerates. *I'm going to hyperventilate.*

I gasp as his weight disappears.

"What the fuck?" Cole's fist slams into Craig's cheek. Craig staggers, and Cole hits him again. There's the longest moment in all of history as seconds pass, and Craig hits the floor hard.

I throw myself at Cole, flinging my arms around his neck as he holds me tight.

"It was Craig," I whisper. "He attacked me here, but I got away."

"Did you remember?"

"Kind of. There are bits. Enough for me to work it out."

"I'm calling the police while he's out and I've got an eye on him." He gives me a kiss on the cheek and pulls his phone out of his pocket. I cling to him while he dials emergency services, my eyes never leaving Craig.

This whole time. All these weeks. He was right under my nose.

My head spins and my knees weaken, but Cole holds me up.

"I'll call Marcus too. Where's your phone?" Cole asks.

"In my bag out the back."

"Go and get it."

I walk around Craig, and run to the back room. Craig's still down as I come back out, and in the distance, I hear sirens.

"Give me your phone. I'll take care of it." He pulls me closer as he dials Marcus. I can barely breathe. My heart's still racing over what just happened. My frustration at not remembering the details of the night I was hit by the car builds, and I shake.

"Hey." Cole hangs up the phone when he finishes his call and hugs me tight.

Three policemen walk through the door. Everything happens in a blur. I answer questions. Marcus arrives. Craig comes around and the police take him away. He glares at me as they drag him out the door.

The whole time, Cole's by my side. He's my strength. He's my rock when everything around me feels like it's falling apart.

When the police are gone, Cole wraps his arms around me, and I press my head against his chest. His heartbeat's familiar and comforting. This is exactly what I need right now.

*Him.*

My breathing steadies, and he kisses the top of my head. "You okay?"

"I am now."

*He's all I need. He's all I've ever needed.*

"Let's get you home."

"Take next week off," Marcus says. "I'm so sorry, Brooke."

"You weren't to know."

He shakes his head. "No. I thought I was a good judge of character."

I snort, and he drops his gaze. "Okay. I know John's a pain in the ass, too."

"He needs to keep his hands to himself, but he did me a favor a while ago."

"I'll put some pressure on him to sort himself out."

I nod. "Thank you."

Grabbing my bag and coat, I walk out the door with Cole. His car's parked outside, and I'm so thankful for the comfort and warmth it provides for the short drive home.

When we get there, Cole walks me into the building and up to my door.

"Want me to come in for coffee?" he asks. "And by that I do mean coffee. I'm not trying anything. Not after what you've been through."

I pat his chest. "As great as that sounds, I just want to take a really long shower and sleep."

He nods.

"I'm not pushing you away, Cole. That's the last thing I want to do. I just need to breathe for a bit."

Cole forces a smile. "I understand. I'll go home now. But you call me if you need anything, and I'll be back later to spend some time with you and Kaia."

I nod. "Thank you."

He runs his index finger along my jawline and raises my face to meet his. His kiss is soft and slow, and I let out a sigh.

"I love you," he says.

My heart skips a beat. My head's still foggy, and I just need some space and sleep.

"Good night, Cole," I whisper.

"Good night. See you later." I open the door. The living room is dark, and for a second I wonder where Rosalyn is.

*Kaia's spending the night at her place.*

Right.

Shower and bed.

---

I CAN'T SLEEP.

I lie in bed, staring at the ceiling. *What the hell am I doing?* I got a fright tonight, but Cole was there. He took care of me and loved me, and I still pushed him away.

He saved me. He was there when I needed him.

He'd already arranged for Craig to walk me home with no plans to pick me up, yet he still turned up. Because he loves me.

And I love him.

I pull out my phone and dial a cab. It's only a few minutes away, so I shoot a quick text to Rosalyn. It's late, but if she doesn't see it tonight, she'll see it in the morning.

After pulling on a pair of jeans and a T-shirt, I head out to the elevator and down to the front of the building.

It's pouring with rain. The water pelts me as I run from the building and into the waiting car. Despite the short distance, the large drops leave me cold and damp. I shiver.

"Are you alright, miss?" the cab driver asks.

I nod. "Let's go."

Settling back into the seat, I close my eyes for a moment. Even if I can't remember before, it's now that matters.

When we pull up outside Cole's house, I hand the driver the money and get out. I run from the car to the front door.

It's exposed, the rain pelting toward it, and there's no relief for me as I knock.

*The first thing I'm going to change about this place is to make sure his door is sheltered.*

His door? Our door. This is my house too. Our family home.

Or at least it will be.

I hammer on the door again, and a light flicks on inside.

"Okay, okay." He pulls open the door, and his eyes drink me in. "Brooke? It's after three in the morning. What are you doing—"

I fling my arms around his neck and crash my mouth onto his. His shoulders slump as he relaxes, kissing me back, his tongue flicking over mine.

We pull apart. Both of us are panting. I need him. I'm so hungry for him that if I waste another minute, I'll starve.

Cole is it. He always was.

"I'll grab you a towel. Come in" He disappears into the bathroom, and when he comes back he attempts to drape a towel over my shoulders. I launch myself at him again, and I'm lost in a tangle of limbs as he takes my demands and fulfills them.

"You're soaking wet." He laughs. "And not in a good way. At least I don't think so."

"Maybe not yet."

His grin lights up the room. He's so happy. "I love it when you talk dirty."

"Take me to bed. I need you. I only need you."

"I thought you'd never ask."

**14**

---

COLE

Is this it? Is this the moment when I get my wife back even without her memory?

I follow her to the bedroom. She comes to a stop at the door.

I scan her expression as I approach. We're nowhere near the point we were before her attack, but there's warmth and, dare I hope, love?

"Are you sure this is what you want?" I ask.

She nods. "I keep having this nagging feeling. It's not a memory, but I know enough to know I should be treating you better. You're Kaia's father, and she loves you so much."

I lick my lips, taking her hands in mine. "What about you?"

"I'm scared. But you haven't backed down once.." She drops her gaze, and her mouth falls open. "You're wearing your wedding ring?"

"I should never have taken it off."

"Cole." Her eyes are so full of emotion.

"You're my wife, Brooke. For better or worse. We've been through the worse." I lean in, giving her a tentative peck. She wraps her arms around my neck, cupping the back of my head and leaving me in no doubt that she wants more.

My tongue strokes hers in long, deliberate moves. She moans, pressing her tight body against me. I'm hard as a rock, and we're both still fully clothed.

I need her naked. I need to suck on the nipples that pebble at my touch. I need to lick my way down her stomach until I find that little piece of heaven between her legs. I need to eat her pussy until she's wet and aching for my cock. And once we've satisfied each other, I'll start all over again.

Reaching down, I pull at her shirt, and she lifts her arms to help me get it over her head. My pants tighten at the sight of her breasts in a plain white cotton bra. It takes me back to that first night together—the night we conceived Kaia.

She gasps when I bend, nipping at her breasts through her bra. I leave wet marks as I suckle on her nipples through the thin fabric.

"Cole," she whimpers.

"Bed."

Grabbing my hand, she pulls me toward the bed. I thought I was happy when we got back together the first time. This time, I'm delirious with joy at the thought of our union. *She doesn't need her memory to know we're right together.*

At the foot of the bed, we stop, and she wraps her arms around my neck, her mouth clashing with mine as we come together with one hot open-mouthed kiss. I roam her body with my hands, pausing at her breasts, and pinching her nipples hard. She lets out a moan.

"Slow, or hard and fast?" I ask.

"You're giving me a choice?" Her breathy laugh makes my cock stir.

"You liked to change it up last time. It's only right I let you choose first."

She laughs against my mouth. "I don't even know. I just want you inside me. Where you belong."

"Is that right?"

She takes a step back, her expression falling. "I'm sorry."

"For what? If you've changed your mind about tonight …"

She shakes her head. "For not having faith."

I shrug. "I understand. It's confusing for all of us. The important thing is that you're safe. I love you."

She reaches behind and unclips her bra, letting it fall to the floor. Her lips curl into a smile as she pushes me backward onto the bed, straddling my hips. "Let's make this right."

"We don't have to do this. You don't have to prove anything to me."

She cocks an eyebrow. "Are you trying to talk me out of sex?"

"No. I just don't want you to think you owe—"

Her mouth covers mine, and she shuts me up with a kiss—one that leaves me in no doubt that she's not just conveying her gratitude. She shrieks as I flip her onto her back on the bed.

"You know how to drive me crazy." I laugh.

"I hope so." Her smile is so beautiful. It lights up her whole being, and I get lost in it for a moment. Is this real? Am I about to get everything I've ever wanted? Everything I thought I had and lost?

She giggles as I pull her panties down her legs and strip off my shirt. I drop my pants to the floor and lie beside her on the bed.

Cupping her pussy, I slip a finger inside. She lets out a small gasp, and I bring my finger up to stroke her clit. Her body shakes as I suck one of her nipples into my mouth. *Hard.*

"Cole," she moans.

I play her clit with my fingers, stroking it gently as I tongue her nipple. She sighs, digging her fingers into my hair. "I love you, Brooke."

"I love you too. I always have." My heart leaps at her words. She falls apart beneath my hand, her hips bucking, her whole body reacting to my touch.

When she shudders, I move between her legs. Her eyes are full of wonder.

I know she can't remember what sex was like between us right before her memory loss, but I'm determined it'll be just as good tonight. We have our connection back.

I run my tongue up each side of her pussy before settling on her clit, teasing her, tasting her until she cries my name and pushes against my face. She's mine again.

Crawling over her, I sink into her hot, tight body, moaning at how wet and soft she is. Nothing has ever felt as right as this. No matter what, Brooke and I belong together. I should have known that from the start.

Maybe she doesn't remember how we fell in love last time, but I'll sure as hell try my best to remind her.

Every day for the rest of my life.

---

WE LIE IN THE AFTERGLOW, and she giggles when I pull her into my arms and pepper her neck with kisses.

"I think we need to get out of bed," I say.

"Why?" she asks.

"Because I'm going to change the sheets and

pillowcases. You should have used that towel. There are drips of water everywhere."

She laughs. "I'll help you."

"Are you warm enough?"

Her eyes shine with contentedness. "I'm very warm. And happy. Happier than I've been in weeks. If I'd known that was all it would take …"

My lips meet hers, and she moans as I give her a deep kiss. "Oh, I can give you lots of that if it makes you happy."

"You make me happy, Cole." She smiles. "And you make Kaia happy. These past few weeks have been miserable, but I think I've worked out what we were missing."

"What?" I play innocent, but I think I know what she's going to say.

"You."

I can't stop myself from grinning. "It's taken you long enough to work that out."

She slaps my arm. "Don't you dare make fun of me."

"I would never do that." I kiss her again, and the sheets are forgotten as I make my wife my own.

In fact, I'm not sure if I'll ever let her out of bed again.

# 15



I LINK my fingers in his as he sleeps—my husband, my love.

I have no regrets this morning, and there's no going back now. Cole and I are together, and nothing will separate us. We've been through a lifetime's worth of pain that's led us back to each other. I think my favorite thing in the whole world is lying here, beside my husband.

When he opens his eyes, I get lost in those dark pools. Kaia shares that trait with him. I've always loved the color of her eyes.

"Morning," he murmurs.

"Good morning."

"Did you sleep well?"

I smile. "Like a log."

"How about I make some coffee and we go and get Kaia?"

My smile widens. "That sounds wonderful. She'll be so happy to see you."

"I just want to be with both of you."

I palm his cheek. "We want to be with you."

Cole slides his arm across me, pulling me toward him. "I could do with another dose of you first, though."

"I won't say no," I whisper.

Closing my eyes, I relax as he covers me in kisses.

I don't know if I've ever been this happy.

———

WE HEAD STRAIGHT to Rosalyn's place when we get to the apartment.

"Brooke. Cole." Rosalyn gives us a warm welcome as she opens the door.

"Hi, Ros," I say.

Kaia runs to the door when she hears my voice.

"Daddy." Kaia jumps up and down. She looks at Rosalyn's granddaughter. "This is my daddy."

"It sure is, baby. You ready to come home?" I ask.

She nods.

"Thank you, Ros."

"It's my pleasure. I got your text."

I nod. "I'd love to catch up later. I'm not working nights next week, so we can get together for coffee if you want."

She smiles. "Well, you still call me if you two

want to go out. It's always a pleasure to take care of Kaia."

"I appreciate it. But I think we'll be spending as much time as we can together for a little while." I suck in a breath. "My attacker was caught last night."

Rosalyn's eyes widen. "That's such good news."

"Cole stopped him." I beam with pride. I'm still a little shaky thinking about it, and Cole slips an arm around my shoulders.

"Are you okay?" Ros says.

I nod. "Thanks to Cole. Maybe we can have coffee during the week."

"That sounds great."

"Anyway, come on, Kaia. We've got some things to talk about," I say. "Thank you for taking care of her."

Kaia grabs hold of Cole's hand while Rosalyn hands me Kaia's bag.

"Thank you." I smile as Rosalyn bends to kiss Kaia goodbye.

It's a short walk home, but it's so good to have the three of us together.

"We have to talk to you, Kaia," I say, leading her to the couch. "Daddy and I are back together." I take a deep breath. "So, we'll be seeing a lot more of him from now on."

Kaia flings her arms around my neck.

"I know you've missed him, sweet girl. He'll never be far away now."

She lets go of me, and does the same to Cole.

He closes his eyes as he hugs her tight. "We're going to spend so much time together, you'll get sick of me."

Kaia laughs. "Daddy."

"I doubt either of us will get sick of you. Not for a while, anyway." I grin.

"I hope not," Cole says.

---

KAIA's like a limpet with Cole. She spends the day glued to his side, barely letting him out of her sight. It warms my heart knowing she won't break down over him leaving because he doesn't have to leave.

After dinner, she falls asleep in his arms. He kisses her on the top of her head.

"Want me to get her changed for bed?" he asks.

I shake my head. "I think this once we'll just tuck her in. It's not going to hurt."

"She's so happy." He strokes her forehead.

"This is all she wanted: you and me together."

He smiles. "I'm glad we are. And not just because of Kaia."

I chuckle. "I should hope not."

"I've never had anyone show up at my house and throw themselves at me."

"Well, I don't do that for just anyone."

His eyes show me just how happy he is. "I should hope not. I'll go and put her into bed."

He's gone for a couple of minutes before returning, and I stand to greet him.

"Let's go to bed."

"I thought I might go home."

I stare at him. "Why?"

"Last night was amazing. But I think I'll leave you and Kaia to have some time together in the morning. After last night, you need it."

"I don't want space anymore, Cole. I want you. Stay, and be her father." I smile. "Stay, and be my husband."

"Are you sure about this?"

"I've never been more sure." I lick my lips. "I'm sorry I've been so distant. Our past hurt me so much, and without my memory, I couldn't see a future."

He smiles. "And now?"

"The only future I see is you."

**16**

———

BROOKE

YESTERDAY WAS the first day we felt like a family again.

My husband spent the whole night showing me how much he loves me. This morning, I wake with him for the second time, and my heart is over-flowing with love.

"Daddy?"

I smile at the sound of Kaia's voice.

"It is Daddy, but you have to be quiet." I raise my free hand to my lips. "He's very tired, and he needs his sleep."

Cole opens one eye.

"Daddy needs a lot of sleep because he's old, and old people need sleep," I finish.

His lips twitch. "I'm not that much older than you."

"A month is a long time. That's four whole weeks."

"Daddy!" Kaia shrieks. She jumps onto the bed and slams herself between us. I move over to give her space while she wraps her arms around his neck and snuggles in against him.

"How about we go and see your room today?" he says.

"Can we?" she asks.

"We need to ask your mother, but I'm sure we can. You'll love it, Kaia." He fixes his gaze on me. "The only question is when you two can move in. I don't want to waste any more time."

I grin. "Neither do I. How about we have breakfast and then go and investigate this room?"

"I'm hungry," Kaia says.

"So am I. I hope there's lots of breakfast in the kitchen for me," Cole says.

She squeals as Cole tickles her, then pulls away and jumps off the bed.

"I'll be there in a minute," I say.

Kaia disappears, and the sound of the television blares when she turns on cartoons.

I lean over, and kiss my husband on the lips. He slides his fingers into my hair and pulls me down hard.

Laughing, I tug away. "What's that for?"

"Calling me old."

"I'll have to do that more often." I kiss him again,

and it would be easy to get lost in him but for the sound coming from the door.

"Mommy."

He lets go of me. "I can't wait to show you the changes I've made at home. The ones you didn't stop to look at when we were there."

"I can't wait to see them. Let's go get some breakfast."

"If you have something to keep her distracted for a while, I'll give you breakfast."

I chuckle as I pull myself off the bed and walk to the door. "There's plenty of time for that, Cole Masters."

"Never enough."

My heart swells as I walk to the kitchen, replaying last night in my mind. I love Cole. I want to be with him for the rest of my life.

There's no turning back now.

***

This house will be our home.

"Go and check out Kaia's room," Cole says.

I take Kaia's hand and lead her up the hallway. I push the door open.

Tears prick my eyes. I didn't come in here last night. Now, I see everything.

Kaia's beloved cartoon characters still cover one wall. The rest of the room is painted pale pink,

Kaia's favorite color. The bed has dark pink blankets.

"Mommy." Kaia's eyes are wide as she looks from one side of the room to the other.

"You did all this?" I turn to ask Cole.

He shrugs. "I had some sleepless nights."

"It's beautiful. Kaia, do you love it?"

"Yes!" She claps. "It's so pretty, Daddy."

I take Cole's hand in mine. "Your daddy is very clever."

He raises my hand to his lips. "My family inspires me. Come here. I've got something else to show you."

My mouth drops when he opens the door to the room next to Kaia's. There's a crib in the corner, with the same characters as the ones in Kaia's room dangling on a mobile. It's painted cream, and has the same nightlight as the one in Kaia's room.

I fight back the tears as he stands behind me and wraps his arms around my waist.

"I'm ready," he murmurs in my ear. "I'm ready for all of it."

"Cole, it's beautiful."

"There are still some finishing touches to do, but I thought you'd like to take care of that." He turns me toward him. "So, when are you moving in?"

I lick my lips. "I'm not sure. Maybe in a few months?"

His eyebrows twitch. "Months?"

I grin. "How about next weekend, then? Is that acceptable? We don't have a lot of stuff."

I laugh as he sweeps me off the floor and into his arms. "I'll sort some movers out. The sooner you two are here, the better."

"And then we'll be three."

Cole nods. "I can't wait."

"There's something I need to tell you too."

His eyebrows rise.

"I'm quitting the bar. And if you'll have me, I'll quit the day job too. I'd like to have some time with Kaia before she starts school. Especially with this baby on the way."

"You got it. We'll be fine." He places me back down. "Now, how about that movie day? I've got some new DVDs and plenty of popcorn."

"Popcorn. Yay!" Kaia comes running into the room.

"Someone's got good hearing." He laughs.

"When she wants to."

Kaia tugs on my shirt. "Mommy. Is this my room too?"

Smiling, I bend and kiss her on the forehead. "No, sweetie. Daddy and I have something to tell you."

I grin at Cole. "Do you want to tell her?"

"Can I?"

I nod.

He picks Kaia up, and carries her over to the crib.

"This is where your baby sister or brother is going to sleep. Until they're big enough for you to play with."

Her mouth falls open. "Baby?"

He nods. "Mommy and Daddy are having a baby, Kaia."

She claps, and I hug both of them. "You're going to be a big sister."

Cole kisses her temple. "How about we go into the living room and start our movie day."

"Sounds like a great idea," I say.

I snuggle with him on the couch, Kaia on his other side. These are the days we'll all cherish forever—the days when we knitted our family together and were what we were always meant to be.

Maybe one day my memory will return, but right now, it doesn't matter if it does or it doesn't.

Love is undeniable between us.

And I've made my peace with the past.

**17**

———————

BROOKE

I'M EXHAUSTED. We don't have a lot of possessions, but moving them from the apartment to the house was tiring. Cole and the movers do the heavy lifting, but packing and unpacking leaves everything aching.

Kaia's over the moon. All the effort is worth it to see the happy smile on her face.

Cole cooks dinner with Kaia helping while I put my feet up.

This is the life I always wanted: the three of us being a family and being happy. I pat my stomach. It'll be the four of us soon enough.

"Brooke, did you want to eat at the table?" Cole asks.

"Do we have to?"

He laughs. "Not at all. I gather you're comfortable there."

"I'd be happy to live on this couch right now."

Cole brings me a plate laden with chicken and mashed potatoes. I groan. "I'm never going to eat all of this."

"You don't have to. But I figured you'd be hungry after today."

"I am."

Kaia sits beside me, a chicken nugget sliding off her plate as she does.

I shake my head. "Be careful."

She picks it up off the floor and pops it in her mouth.

Kaia giggles. It's good to see her so happy. No more crying for daddy because he's right here. She dips the next chicken nugget in ketchup, and I bite down a laugh as it's smeared over her mouth.

I look down at her. "You can have your bath after dinner."

Kaia pouts.

Cole grins. "I can make it with bubbles."

Her eyes widen. "Bubbles?"

"I'm sure there's something in the bathroom that'll make some bubbles." He moves his gaze to me. "We could have a bath before bed too."

I grin. "I love that idea."

"We can't all fit in the bath." Kaia giggles.

We burst out laughing.

"No, we can't." I shake my head. "Eat your dinner.'

She smiles, and picks up another chicken nugget.

When we're finished, Cole collects the plates. I

protest, feeling the need to do something, anything, but he won't let me. He kisses me tenderly, and leaves to fill the dishwasher.

I have the perfect man. Even if I feel useless.

Cole comes back after a few minutes. "Come on, Kaia. Let's get you bathed and ready for bed."

She rounds the couch and disappears up the hallway with Cole.

I look around. Cole's taken care of everything. There's nothing for me to do. I could get used to this. At least, for a while.

I pick up the television remote and turn on the TV. Flicking through the channels, I settle on the news. It's enough to keep my mind occupied for half an hour, though bed is calling.

Kaia runs into the room, this time dressed in her pajamas.

"Good night, Mommy." She hugs me tight, and I close my eyes, just breathing her in. Seeing her happy is everything.

"Good night, sweet girl." I kiss the top of her head.

She jumps down from the couch and takes Cole's hand.

"I'll read you a story, and you go straight to sleep. Okay?" he asks.

"Can we have the star lights?"

"Of course we can."

I sigh contentedly as they walk up the hallway.

There was such a long time when I would never have believed this—that we could be a family again. Yet here we are, in our new home for a fresh start.

I close my eyes. The thought of a hot bath with Cole is wonderful, but sinking into that soft bed is even more appealing.

"She's fast asleep."

I jump. I've never been one for falling asleep just anywhere, but while Cole was busy putting Kaia to bed, I think I was nearly out to it.

"That didn't take long."

"It's been a long day for all of us." He sits beside me on the couch. "Happy?" Cole asks, nuzzling my ear.

"Very."

I yawn, and he laughs. "Am I keeping you up?"

*I know what I'd like to be keeping up, but I'm so tired I don't think sex is on the cards.*

"I don't think I'll be much good for anything except sleeping tonight."

He drops his head to nuzzle my neck, and I sigh.

"You are such a distraction."

"That's the aim." He laughs against my skin. "I love that you're here."

"I love you."

He pulls away. "Let's renew our vows."

I grin, and my mouth falls open as he drops to one knee in front of me and pulls a small box out of his pocket.

"I presume you have your wedding ring some-where, and I never bought you an engagement ring the first time with everything being so rushed." He takes a deep breath. "So, I got you this."

He opens the box, and inside is a diamond soli-taire ring.

"Cole, it's beautiful."

He takes it out of the box. "It's a symbol of how much I love you."

Tears prick my eyes when he slips it on my ring finger and it's a close fit. "Wait. How did you do that?"

"Took a guess with the help of a woman in the jewelers. I got it a while ago, but now seemed like the time to give it to you."

I laugh. "I can't wait to tell Kaia."

He nods. "Me too. She'll be so excited. No registry office this time." Cole moves up from the floor to the couch. "There'll never be anyone else for me, Brooke. There never has been. You're the one who makes me want to be a better person, and my heart belongs to you."

I reach for his face, palming his cheek. "I love you."

"I love you too."

We're going to be a family again.

And this time it will last.

Because this time, there's real love.

# EPILOGUE
## COLE

"Nervous?" Dad asks as I fiddle with my cufflinks. I hate these things, but I wanted Brooke to have the wedding she always wanted. It's not like we had a fancy wedding last time around.

"Very. It's crazy. You'd think the second time would be easier."

He smiles, and grips my shoulder. "You're doing it for love this time. Oh, I know you two loved each other before, but you married Brooke out of a sense of duty. This time's different."

I nod. "When did you get to be so wise?"

"When I realized just how many mistakes I made back then. I'll never forgive myself for the way I treated Brooke."

"She's forgiven you."

"That's because your wife is a very understanding woman. She reminds me of her father so much. I don't know if there's really any doubt about her paternity."

I smile. "Would it matter?"

Dad shakes his head. "No. I'll treat her like a daughter no matter what. The way she should have been treated."

"Thanks, Dad."

"You make me so proud, Cole."

For the first time in a long time, we feel united and strong.

I didn't just get Brooke and Kaia back to become a family. Everyone I love has all come together.

And today is just the icing on the cake.

---

THE BACKYARD HAS a small group of chairs in front of a floral arch. We didn't want anything fussy, but we wanted to make this wedding more of an occasion than the first.

The people we love are all here. Mike and Liz, who are dating now, sit waiting along with Katie, Eric, Marcus, and even sour Jenny. Brooke wanted to invite the people who had made a difference in our lives, and they all fit the bill. Rosalyn's here with her daughter.

I grin as I walk through the middle of our friends and family to the celebrant.

"Ready?" The celebrant asks.

"As I'll ever be."

Somehow, Brooke put all this together in the past month, and it's beautiful. She's radiant with joy, and she's looking rested and stress-free for the first time since I found her again. I'm sure a lot of it comes from her being able to spend more quality time with Kaia. This new baby will get all of her.

And all three of them will get all of me.

I look up as the music plays.

When I see her, she takes my breath away.

She walks down the aisle toward me, and there's no father to give her away. Brooke radiates in her short bright yellow dress as she approaches me bathed in sunlight. She wanted today to be full of light and happiness to set the tone for our future life.

Kaia's dress is a bright blue.

Brooke's hand in hand with Kaia, and our little girl has a smile as big as her mother's. They both have eyes just for me. It's overwhelming. I don't know which of my girls to look at.

Tears are in my eyes by the time Brooke takes my hand.

"You look beautiful," I whisper.

I shift my gaze to Kaia, who's standing on the other side of Brooke. "You look beautiful too."

Kaia giggles and swings on her heels, and her cheeks grow pink. "Daddy."

I smile as Kaia shuffles between us. This is what we wanted. Our whole family together.

"Good morning, everyone. I'm Cathy Simmons, the celebrant, and I'm honored to be here to celebrate the renewal of Brooke and Cole's wedding vows." She smiles. "This is going to be a really special ceremony as Brooke and Cole reaffirm their love for one another, and afterward the couple wish to invite you inside for food and drinks to celebrate."

She turns to me. "Cole. Would you like to share your vows with Brooke?"

I nod. We wanted to keep this brief as Brooke's still struggling with the fatigue of pregnancy. This one's hit her harder than her pregnancy with Kaia did, and while we're so close to telling the world about the baby, it'd be nice to keep it to ourselves for just a little longer.

"Brooke, every morning I wake up feeling blessed. To have you back in my life has made me complete, and I promise I will cherish each and every day with you. You're the best thing that ever happened to me."

She tears up, and I let go of one hand and catch the tears one by one with my index finger as they escape down her cheeks.

"Brooke?" The celebrant prompts.

Brooke breathes in deep, and licks her lips. "I love you, Cole. I have done since we were five years' old, and you pinky promised to be my best friend forever. We took the rocky road to be here, but the only thing that matters is that we are here, and we're together."

It's clear she's struggling, and I squeeze her hands.

"Today, Cole is not only making promises to Brooke. He also has some things to say to their daughter, Kaia."

Brooke shuffles behind Kaia, a wide grin on her face. I look down at my daughter and clear my throat. Taking her hand in mine, I kneel in front of her. "I, Cole, promise to always be a good daddy. I'll be there whenever you need me to be. No matter how old you get. I love you, Kaia."

The small congregation gives us a collective *awww* as my daughter throws her arms around my neck.

"Love you, Daddy," she says.

I stand, lifting Kaia with me. Brooke hugs both of us, and for a moment there's no one else around. Just the three of us.

*My family.*

---

Kaia waves goodbye as she gets into the car with Mom and Dad. They're staying at a nearby hotel, and had already offered to take her for the night when she got wind of where they were staying. She wanted to visit their little house again. I hope she's not too disappointed it's a different hotel.

It'll be weird not to have her around. While Brooke and I have been looking forward to peace and quiet, Kaia's presence is everywhere.

The one thing I am glad for is getting the chance at a second wedding night. One where Brooke feels loved and wanted. The one she should have had in the first place.

There'll be no awkwardness between us this time.

"I'm impressed you're trusting my parents with Kaia." I kiss her again, lingering on those sweet lips.

"Who said I trusted them? I trust *you*." Her blue eyes shine with happiness.

"I've waited a long time to hear you say that."

She nods. "Like I said, we took the rocky road. But I'm glad we've reached the end."

I look around the room. Most of the food went quickly, and the small amount that's left is tucked away for us to eat tomorrow. We said goodbye to everyone leaving dishes to be done, and crumbs to vacuum up, but I'll take care of that tomorrow while my wife recovers from wedding night sex.

*The best kind.*

"Should we clean up?" Brooke asks.

"No. Leave it. We've got other more important things to do."

She smiles. "Like what?"

Taking her hand, I lead her toward the bedroom. "I want to set the world record for the number of times I've been inside my wife in a single night."

Brooke throws her head back and laughs. "We both know I'll be asleep by ten."

"Well, we'd better get started then."

---

I LIE ON MY BACK.

Her blond hair hangs in curls around her face, and I wrap one lock around my index finger, pulling her down to kiss me. "I love you."

"I love you too." She leans back. Her breasts are already bigger thanks to the pregnancy. Was she like this with Kaia? I'm ashamed not to remember.

Her hips jolt me into life as her pussy closes around my cock. Once upon a time, I thought we'd never reach this level of love and trust again. Now it wraps us in its warm glow, and feeds my need for her.

She thrusts hard, taking me deep inside her, and I smile at the look of concentration on her face.

"You're just going to take what you need, aren't you?"

A sly smile crosses her lips. "I need everything."

"Just as well I have everything to give."

And then I'm lost, surrounded by the woman I

love. I might have lost four years with her, but I'll never lose another second.

She presses her hands to my pecs, grinding her hips until I let out a moan. I'm floating on the wave of this climax, gripping her body tight against mine. Her eyes widen with her own, and I smile at the strain on her face when she comes. I could do this all night.

She rolls to my side, and I take her in my arms and kiss her. *Long. Slow. Deep.* A sigh catches in her throat, and I drop my lips to her neck to follow it.

"Cole." Her loving tone fills my heart. "I'd like to get some sleep now."

"If you weren't pregnant, I'd do my best to keep you awake." I chuckle. Laying my palm on her stomach, I smile at the thought of our growing baby. This is a symbol of our renewed love, and he or she will be the center of our universe, along with big sister Kaia.

"I'm glad I have an excuse to snooze." She yawns. "No, not really. I'd much rather fool around with you all night."

"We'll have plenty of other nights. A lifetime of them."

Brooke raises her hand to stroke my cheek. "Thank you for today."

"It was for all of us."

"Your promise to Kaia was so sweet. I hope she remembers that for the rest of her life."

"Me too." I suck in a breath. "As nice as it is not to have to worry about her bursting in here, I miss her."

Brooke laughs. "So do I. It's like I have a missing limb when she's not around."

I run my index finger down her neck, all the way to her nipple. She gasps when I pinch it. "Are you really sure you need to sleep?"

A sly smile crosses her lips. "I think I just got a better offer."

"I love you, wife."

"Love you too, husband."

This couldn't be any more different to our first wedding night.

Two souls have finally become one, united in the love that we kept coming back to, no matter how many barriers were put between us.

My love for Brooke trumps everything.

It's for life.

Always growing.

Always rising.

*Pinky promise.*

# ALSO BY WENDY SMITH

Coming Home

Doctor's Orders

Baker's Dozen

Hunter's Mark

Teacher's Pet

A Very Campbell Christmas

Fall and Rise Duet

Falling

Rising

Fall and Rise - The Complete Duet

The Aeon Series

Game On

Build a Nerd

Bar None

Hollywood Kiwis Series

Common Ground

Even Ground

Under Ground

Rocky Ground

Solid Ground

Stand alones
For the Love of Chloe
Only Ever You

The Friends Duet
Loving Rowan
Three Days

The Forever Series
Something Real
The Right One
Unexpected

Chances Series
Another Chance
Taking Chances

Lifetime Series
In a Lifetime
In an Instant
In a Heartbeat
In the End
At the Start

# ABOUT THE AUTHOR

Wendy Smith lives with her two children and three cats in Hastings, New Zealand, and she's not sure who's responsible for her grey hair. She's a multi-platform bestselling author, whose book In the End, written as Ariadne Wayne, was named one of Apple's best books of 2017. All her stories come with a quirky sense of humour, and she cries over everything.

*Find me online*
www.wendysmith.co.nz
wendy@wendysmith.co.nz

www.ingramcontent.com/pod-product-compliance
Lightning Source LLC
Chambersburg PA
CBHW020806310726
48969CB00002B/725